LIMINAL DOMESTIC

Marsh,

Thank you for every good
conversation, every word you shared
with me, and for keeping me sane
some days when I needed it.
So so so proud of you.

-Zach

LIMINAL DOMESTIC: STORIES
Zach VandeZande

for you, maybe

CONTENTS

SOME THINGSOME THING

Something is coming for you. We are not at liberty to say what. At a certain point it does not matter what it is, just that it's coming for you and it's big. Not bigger than you, maybe, but big enough. And with claws, or jaws, or a reticulated pattern going down its back. One of those at least, but likely more. Likely it will arrive at your door and the door will not stop it. Likely you will realize that doors are in some ways a matter of decorum, if you have time to realize, if you are even aware at all, as something often comes in the night, or at you sideways, or through your subconsciousness, or it doesn't come at all and instead leaves you there to deal with yourself, which is the worst one.

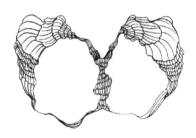

LIMINAL DOMESTIC

A squirrel, a raccoon, a family of mice: something must have died in the walls of the house. It filled the bedroom with alien rot, curled up Beck's top lip, her smile one of disgust.

"What the fuck is that smell?" she asked.

"I don't smell anything," Mark said, "and language, come on, Beck." He was playing with the baby, Turner. There were floppy stuffed animals arranged in rows on the bed. Mark turned to them and said, "Ladies and gentleman of the jury, my client is innocent!" He whirled toward Turner, who squealed with glee. Mark would be trying the bar again in February.

Beck went around the room sniffing. Turner stood up and wobbled behind her. Beck had taken to strategically ignoring him, which he tolerated just fine, far better than Mark did. She said it was to foster independence, but really she worried she might come unglued from answering Turner's every need, and she needed these little rebellions against motherhood. Her biceps were huge from carrying her child, and she thought she might disappear.

The smell was strongest near the head of the bed, on the south wall. It had been an unusually warm few weeks, lots of Texas sunshine even this deep into fall, and whatever it was seemed to be baking in the walls.

The smell radiated. She bent down and stuck her head between the bed and the dresser. Her nose was thick with it, piss and rot. She suppressed a gag. There was a heat to it, the smell a kind of lure, drawing her in underneath all the vileness. She stood up.

"Here," she said to no one. Turner tripped over one of Mark's loafers and began to scream.

．．．

Mark worked four days a week at a small firm, prepping casework and repeatedly explaining to senior partners how the copy machine worked. He was doggedly ambitious, but made no secret of how much he hated the work. He and Beck did their best to avoid the reality of the situation: that if he'd passed the bar he wouldn't be there, that if her pregnancy hadn't been so fraught with depression and an unexpected onset of preeclampsia—Beck had always been healthy, a runner—he might've had more time to study for the bar, that if they had stuck to their plan of waiting until he was thirty-two and she was thirty to have a child they wouldn't have the added burden of a house payment. On and on, and no getting out of it now. At night in bed together, the baby monitor hissing slightly, one or the other of them would say, "We got here entirely on purpose." And it was true, or true enough.

That night, Beck lay awake until the early hours, the smell gnawing at her. Eventually she got up and tromped around the room by the light of her phone, searching. It seemed to be both everywhere she wasn't and also emanating from her, or at least stuck to her skin. Yet when she left the room, it was gone.

Eventually her investigation woke Mark. "What are you doing?" he asked.

"You really don't smell that?"

"I don't. Go to sleep. I'll have the guy come out and look."

Beck hated the guy. He was a craggly, gnomish misogynist of a maintenance man who always found a way to make her feel stupid even as she knew that he was basically less than a nobody to her. Mark's response to him was to shrug and say *Some people are assholes, nothing to do about it.*

"Don't call the guy. It's fine. Get some sleep."

Mark was already out, though. She thought she might sleep on the couch, but she didn't. She wandered the room until dawn.

On two of the days Mark was at work, Turner went to a daycare that masqueraded as an early development center for gifted babies. There was no standard of admission—any baby whose family could afford it was considered gifted. Most days, she would spend a few hours afterward wandering the aisles of a grocery store or a Target, picking up items and dropping them into a cart. More often than not, she would abandon the half-filled cart along the way and leave with the one or two items she really needed. It was meditative, the filling up and then the letting go.

After dropping Turner off Monday morning, she went instead to a hardware store. At first she wasn't sure what she was doing there, what solution she hoped to find, so she drifted through the store like she would any other. She passed pallets of wood, the rainbow of paint samples all agleam, the senseless specificity of each different type of screw and bolt and washer, all of it unknown to her, so very far from her understanding of *house* while still being exactly what a house was made of.

It was the sledgehammer that stopped her. She stared at it for a moment in all its dumb potential before hoisting it off the rack and placing it head down in front of her. It came up to her chest. She put her hands on the smoothed wood—a sensible, unpainted handle that suggested an urgency and simplicity of purpose. She thought that a person with a sledgehammer would know everything they need to know.

She picked it up. She found gloves in one aisle, goggles in another. As she walked through the store with the sledge hoisted over her shoulder, she felt like she might and could do anything at all.

She passed a woman and her three-year-old daughter trying to pick out a bird feeder and seed. The woman would hold one up and say *Well what do you think? What do you think, darling? Which one would the birds like? Are you excited to see the birds?* Beck thought if she swung the hammer around with all her strength, the whole city block might fall down around them.

Back home, she moved everything into one corner of the bedroom, kicking stuffed animals, a blanket, a breast pump into a heap. She wiggled the oak nightstand out of the way, braced herself against the bed, and pushed it aside. Underneath was a dead cockroach and a condom wrapper with a used condom stuffed inside. She picked them up with a paper towel. They made the same sound between her fingers, both desiccated and dust-fluffed.

With everything out of the way, the smell was stronger, thick enough to blot out thought. Beck lost access to herself beyond being a body, a stink-led mammal working on instinct.

She brought the hammer down in a wide pendulum swing. It struck the wall hard and went through easily. She felt a little spark of joy in her. She raised the hammer high and swung it down again, making a ragged hole to the left of the first. She swung again, and the drywall cracked wide, joining the two holes.

She waited, thinking some skeletal starving thing might come scrabbling out at her or a horde of teeming insectile filth. But nothing moved except the dust swirling, the ragged air in her chest. She raised the sledge and swung again.

She kept swinging. Dust cut across the sunlight slanting into the room. It was like something was pouring out from the wall and into her, from the hammer up into her arms. Each swing's moment of connection was an answer thunking at her core.

When she was done, she let the hammer fall. She knelt down and looked at the wound she'd made, a hole about the size of her child. She thought if she worked at it she could squeeze on through. She was sweaty, coated with sheetrock dust.

She couldn't see anything dead in there by the light of her cell phone screen. The emergency flashlights that her father had bought her every third or fourth Christmas since she turned eighteen were all in the closet, unplugged and uncharged. The smell seemed muted since she'd begun hammering, and she wondered if it was actually lessening or if adrenaline had distorted her perception or if maybe the smell was imagined.

She shimmied into the hole, a shark born in reverse.

For dinner she made spaghetti. She'd cleaned up the mess, covered the hole with the dresser. It had been hot inside the wall. When she got in there, she felt gingerly around at the sheetrock, the studs. Her palm grazed an exposed nail. She pressed her back to the outer wall of the house and pushed against the inner wall with her hands, stretching out the tensed, knotty muscles of her back. The air smelled faintly of mold. There was no dead animal that she could tell.

At the kitchen table, Beck felt like she'd left at least half of herself back in the wall. Turner grabbed some spaghetti with a fat fist and flung it. He could play with spaghetti for hours. Beck would nurse him later, after dinner. Mark was saying something about client liability. Beck thought of being in the wall. She could feel herself going a little flush. She squeezed her legs together and tried to think of something else. Behind her the living room, all that wild space. She thought *There is a used diaper on the coffee table. You left it there.*

It was a tight fit. As she made her way sideward through the wall, she felt carefully for anything that might cut, splinter, bruise. She braced herself with each footstep. She wasn't afraid of injury but of giving herself away. Mark was a thoroughly reasonable man. It made him a good husband, but not much for indulgence in mystery.

Passing each stud required her to suck in, chafed her tender breasts. She couldn't say why she was doing this, but what was the point in saying everything all the time? Words were such ugly things, dividing the world into true and not true. In the wall, words didn't carry the sense they normally did. There just wasn't enough room for them. She made herself smaller by letting them go, was able to squeeze beyond the studs one by one, part of her knowing she should go back, the rest of her knowing she should go on. The air was dry. It scratched at her throat. She stopped and listened, smelled. Sweat carved its way down her dirty limbs. There nothing else in here with her. There was barely even her anymore.

If she reached out, she could feel a place where the path

9

inside the wall diverged. She could either continue around the edge of the house or explore one of the inner walls. She wanted very much to do both at once.

That night the smell returned. By then she'd explored enough to know that there wasn't anything actually in the wall. All she'd discovered was the smell of cut wood and mildew, the bones of the house, the stillness of air long unbreathed. She was the only thing that had ever moved in the wall. She rolled over in bed and put her head to the hole and inhaled. If anything the smell had grown. Her nostrils burned, and she put a hand behind the dresser, feeling the chalky edges. The wall felt brittle and fibrous near the hole. How strange, the things we think are solid.

She went into the other room and woke Turner, kissed his feather-haired head, and took him into her room, hoping he would notice the smell too. But he grabbed at her breast and put his head down, went back to sleep in her arms. She bounced him aggressively, brought his face down near the hole. He didn't react at all except to smile at this new game, like *What a silly mommy.* He was normally such a sensitive boy.

She pinched his leg then, harder than she should've. He went still in her arms, and there was a moment where it seemed like nothing would happen next. Then the boy began to wail, and his cries brought on something heavy in her, not guilt but grief. Mark stirred, and she hurried the boy to the living room and cried right along with him, shushing him, promising to make it better. Promising all of herself and more.

. . .

She got to where she knew exactly where she was between the rooms of the house. Here the bathroom, here the garage, here pipes that ran from guest bath to kitchen that she had to straddle awkwardly. Once she got her foot stuck for half an hour, thirty minutes of panic before she was able to continue. Though time wasn't really the same in the wall. It slowed. She'd set the alarm clock each morning and place it facing the hole, a beacon that went off in the mid-afternoon, giving her time to move the furniture back and clean up and get Turner as though they'd been together all day.

The secret of it thrilled her. She had been secretless for years, since when she and Mark had first dated and she'd quit smoking for him. Not that he ever asked her to. She just knew he hated it, and she knew he was a worrier. One day she said *Hey, I quit smoking*, and his face lit up and he kissed her and said he was so proud. She kept smoking at work and around certain friends for about eight months after that day. When he caught her, he didn't even get angry. He just looked at her with a crestfallen face and said *Oh*. It was far too sincere to be manipulative. And that was that. No more smoking.

Turner had an earache and had to stay home. Beck put medicine in his ears, rocked him while he wailed, let him nurse unending. His fever was bad enough that his eyes were wild and blank while he looked up at her, but the thermometer said he was okay and her pediatrician had recently retired without warning. She'd yet to find another, and the burden of it seemed both silly and far too immense. When he finally fell asleep, she put him in his crib and stood at the entrance to the wall, waiting for permission that wouldn't come. She thought if she could just hold her breath long enough it might stop time entirely. She knelt down near the hole and did something sort of like praying. The smell was there like always, but it had changed, become a part of her life instead of an intrusion into it. Still it made her uneasy and ill, an intolerable part of her that she only knew one way to escape.

She entered the wall, made her way as quickly as she could to Turner's room, and listened. She thought she could feel him on the other side, in his crib, fists balled at the sides of his head like he was still a newborn, which he always did when he had a fever. She settled in where she stood. She waited for either his cries or for something more real to happen.

That night, Mark came in holding Turner while Beck was peeing. "You closed the door," he said, as though the fact were absurd. Turner was wet-faced and ruddy.

"I did."

He frowned. "Where's the koala?"

Beck bit down hard on the inside of her cheek. "The fucking koala?"

Turner started up again. There were scratches on Beck's arms, and she crossed them as though she was angry to hide the marks. And she was angry, though she couldn't say at what.

In the wall Beck gave in to wave after wave of memory. Once she was in love with only herself. Once she was this horrible crashing comet of a girl. Once she would check herself in the mirror, drunk with a fake ID, and say *You. Yes, you.* and then smile wide with dazzling teeth. Once she was pregnant and got to be more than and then even more than herself, before she became less. Once she was sure of her ability to affect change in the world, to pick up a glass of water and have it actually rise up off the table to her lips. It's so strange, living every single day of a life. It makes no sense whatsoever.

She forgot herself and edged further and further from the hole. Once a man filled up a woman's heart, and then a little boy, and she let them claim more and more of her. Once a woman was glad to give every bit of herself away, and still it would be wrong to say the woman regretted doing it, because she didn't. She only wished to be back in that time when she was able to give and give, when it was the only thing there was to do.

Once there was a desiccated something in the wall, and a hammer, and a woman who could feel her way forward but not see.

Beck sunk down as far as she could, her knees banging the drywall, ending in a kind of half squat. She could lie down sideways, but she wasn't sure if she'd be able to get up again. She stayed that way for hours, sweat dripping down the small of her back and off her nose.

Outside the wall, the smell of dead things nearly made her retch. In the wall, there was only dry air, though it smelled strongest of death at the entrance to the wall. As she got a few feet away in either direction, it faded entirely. She spent the morning and most of the afternoon feeling her way along until she ended up either somewhere near the bathroom or the baby's room. She was far enough away from the entrance to be in utter darkness. The air was musty. Something crunched when she shifted her foot. A peace came over her that felt like longing. In the distance, through the wall, the child.

While Turner was napping, Mark came home and she undid his belt and pushed him down on the couch. She felt wild, a little dangerous, like when they'd first been dating and she'd goaded Mark into doing it in several public places, including an IHOP bathroom and in a back corner of his law school library. He always needed a little convincing that it was okay to give in to this kind of thing. She found it endearing, but it bothered her how rarely these kinds of moments were his idea.

She pressed herself down on him, pushing his shoulders back into the couch cushion. It was a thread-worn couch they got on Craigslist, and it groaned beneath them. Beck tried to let go, tried to immerse herself fully in the moment, but she couldn't. A part of her wasn't there. She closed her eyes and pictured the things she couldn't see when she was in the wall. In the wall she felt weightless, devoid of hard things like tooth or bone. In the wall she was her own secret. This is what she was thinking when she came.

At night, after Mark and the baby had gone to sleep, Beck sat quietly in bed listening to her own breathing. She reached an arm up and tapped the wall softly with a knuckle. From inside the wall, Beck tapped back. A peace settled over everything, and the house breathed softly all together.

. . .

She spent the day entirely in the wall. She took Turner to daycare again that morning, though it wasn't a scheduled day. She claimed a doctor's appointment and handed the wailing boy over. Her heart broke clean in half like always, but the smell had overpowered her on waking. She thought, if anything, it was becoming more powerful. She refused to believe that the smell might be psychosomatic or that it might be something of her own making. In the wall she thought about sense, about the phrase *making sense,* and how it admitted to a kind of creation in the interpretation of reality. Mark still didn't smell anything.

That evening she avoided the bedroom so she wouldn't give herself away. Mark hardly noticed. He was busy doting on Turner, studying, and diddling with his phone. She grew annoyed by his not noticing, as though she were a child playing mental hide-and-seek with him. After the sun was fully set, she got her headphones and went into the garage for her running shoes and then walked out the front door without a word. It was so humid her phone screen was slicked with moisture. She couldn't get it to respond to her touch, couldn't set any music to play. But it didn't matter, because when she looked up from it and at her neighborhood her breath caught. The world was so large and dark. The starlight came from a time before she existed, before she was even an idea of a person. How could a person enter into this without being flattened by the enormity of it all?

She ran back to the garage and wept, her palms flat against the wall, her forehead pressed against it. Then she curled her fingers up, scraping away a bit of drywall with her nails, and then she was scratching, and her lip turned up into a snarl, and she was clawing at the wall the way an animal would, leaving deep gouges with her nails, knowing that something was wrong, that she was too brittle, or too combustible, or something else, and she needed to get away, and what was there to do but keep burrowing into the wall, and then a fingernail bent back and broke, sending a small shock of pain up her finger, and she stopped.

Beck came back to herself. The damage to the wall was plainly visible and at eye level. There would be no hiding it, and any excuse she came up with would be thin. Catching herself while falling, an animal loose in the garage—anything she could think of was too obviously a lie. If and when Mark asked, there would be only one true thing: *I don't know*. It would start an unraveling between them, but there was nothing different she could say.

Mark ate his breakfast over a textbook. When Beck walked in with Turner, he looked up and said, "I slept weird. My legs feel funny. I think I pinched a nerve on the couch the other day."

Beck tapped the book. "You're just nervous." She went to the counter and poured herself a cup of coffee. She shifted Turner away from her free hand and took a sip, and the rich warmth of it flooded into her. She realized how much she'd missed it these past two years.

Mark grimaced. "What about him?"

"He'll be fine." She headbutted the boy, who smiled. "Won't you? Just a little secondhand caffeine. You'll be bright-eyed in daycare and nap a little later, once you're back home, yeah?"

"Daycare? It's Wednesday."

Beck took another sip of coffee. "Huh. I thought it was Thursday. Probably I need this more than I thought."

Mark made his *be careful* face and looked back to his textbook. After a second, he said, "Did you ever figure out that smell?"

Beck's shoulders tensed up. "Are you telling me you smelled it?"

"No, but who knows. Should I call someone?"

"No. It went away." Somewhere between the bathroom and living room, Beck felt herself sigh in relief.

As soon as Mark left, she set to work. Took Turner to daycare. She didn't bother with an excuse. She just handed him over. Drove back home, creeping past the line at every stoplight, her left foot bouncing. Ate the remains of a soggy bowl of cereal in the kitchen. Cleaned it, cleaned the kitchen, cleaned the whole house. Moved the dresser just enough to get into the hole, then pulled it close to the wall behind her.

In the darkness she could breathe and be real. She made her way forward, determined to search every nook, every dead end, to climb over the door frames and under the window mountings and fully know her home. It was rough going, and she quickly became knee-scraped and filthy, but it was also exhilarating. With each obstacle passed, each corner turned, she felt closer to the thing inside the wall.

There was a light, pale and wintry. Beck couldn't tell how far it was or what it might be, but she kept edging toward it, an inch at a time. It seemed the walls had been getting tighter, trying to bar her progress. The studs hugged her so snugly now that she often found herself not touching the ground at all as she pulled herself through. The light didn't seem to grow any brighter, but it seemed larger, more of a presence around her. The dead darkness became a cave-lit murk. The dry air thickened.

Beck thought of saying something there in the wall, but couldn't find anything. She was slicked with sweat. Her clothes were torn and filthy. Her mouth burned, ragged with thirst and need.

The walls began tearing at her clothes and she pressed on. The time for caution had passed. Suddenly the space widened, and she was able to walk facing forward. Behind her, she could hear the sounds of the house, of her husband arriving home with the baby. She could hear her name, and she ran. Her muscles, stiff and achy from the effort of squeezing through the tight spaces, loosened. As she ran, things unfurled behind her—first her clothes, which went to tatters from the force of her motion. Then her hair, which came off in strands and then great locks, lost in the liminal space between the wall, which had widened out so much that it seemed infinite. Her skin came away, making her fingers look like linnaeas in bloom before flaking off in papery sheets. The muscle began loosening and peeling back in fibrous strands. Still she ran, because the running was there. Time flowed in both directions as she ran, and the ground wore away at her bones until she fell, her crumbling feet kept together by the ligaments, scraps of skin, and little else. She kept on, nails and elbows. There was screaming behind her, the howl of loss and a need for relief. She joined in as she crawled on. Ahead of her was the light, and she could see herself there in it, reaching out, a Beck at once bounded and infinite and whole, a Beck never forced to the precipice of decision, but also Beck herself, the Beck she had become, and all she had to do was get to the light. She scrabbled onward, through the pain and the splintering of bone. And when she did finally reach the source of the light, when she found the hole leading outside, when she took hold of the outstretched hand and scrabbled out into the evening wild, while far away she could hear the sounds of her house come alive with panicked father and broken child, there was nothing at all left of her.

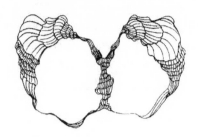

The baby got born wrong. No one cared to say it to the mother. After all she'd been through, we felt she deserved to see the baby her way, tell the baby's story as hers. The pain faded, the baby thrived, the world took little notice of another creature, strange though it was.

When the doctor said the baby was healthy and that they could leave, the father winced. He thought of his wife—that night he found her on the rocky shore of the lake, her soaking wet and shivering. Before then, he'd always thought of unclothed bodies as naked, a word that told it like it was some pedestrian and idiot way to be. She taught him better with her body, the completedness of it in moonlight.

The horns were velvety nubs on each side of the baby's forehead. They weren't a danger. At nap time, the baby would reach up and hold them, a faint smile on its lips. The father watched the baby often while it slept. He didn't know what he expected to see. Something of him. Something for loving right.

The baby grew, and it grew.

Once, the baby yawned and a bee drifted from its mouth, tracing lazy arcs through what was the father's office. The father was there to see it. He watched with dread as the bee jounced along the wall. It was silent as it went and slowing. The father was anticipating something. He didn't know what. The bee settled onto the changing table, splayed its legs, and died.

The baby began to cry. The baby clutched its horns and would not stop crying. The piercing staccato of that. What it is to be this kind of alive, when the bee first leaves you by its bumbling.

PRIMOGENITIVE

One day she squirreled herself away into a word.

It was like the word was a box and she got in it. Or it was like a crack just big enough. Or it was like a deep well, and the word was the lip of the well, and the meaning was the rest— as in the depth and the stone dropped-and-kerplunking and the absence of light—and she became the meaning.

It was a good trick. That is to say, I don't know how it was done. We were eating dinner, and we'd been a little unhappy. It was August. We always seemed to be unhappy then. Just a little. And I'd said something that I meant as both funny and not funny about our unhappiness. Which was a thing I did. She called it *the mask of not wearing a mask*. It was one of my bigger problems.

Anyway I said this thing. Just a tossed off thing. Unmeant. And also of course meant. And she grabbed one of the words from the thing I'd said out of the air and was gone.

And she didn't come out for a long time. And then: she never came out. I sat there holding the word in my mind for a long time. Or: I thought the word once, and then didn't think another thought for a long time. This went on for a good bit, and then I thought of what to do: I would eat the word. Swallow it. Keep her safe, or me, or us both, until the time came.

And somewhere a man decides that when the girl next to him wakes up he will marry her.

And somewhere else a woman tells a man that it's okay, that he can go, and he sits on the porch a little while before he does.

And somewhere else a man really figures something out about himself, and it feels to him like he's having a thought for the very first time.

And somewhere a person who is too old to eat over the sink eats dinner over the sink.

And somewhere people are dying. And somewhere else people die. And somewhere besides that people die. On and on.

And but here I am telling you about making a meal of a word so that it matters against these other things. What I did was I held the word in my mouth like I was going to say it and then swallowed. So that it could never be spoken again. At least not by me. But I expect not by everyone else, too. I expect I changed the world.

The word didn't get digested in the usual way. Instead it was absorbed. It made its way into my bloodstream. It got lodged somewhere in my heart. And I thought: how cliché. And I thought: I can feel it. And I thought: don't feel it. And I thought the word.

So I had this word in my heart. And for a while it rattled around, and I had a paint-can heart. But then that stopped, because the word grew, and I could feel it against the muscles. The muscles pressed on it and gave it shape. So I guess I had an oyster heart. But it wasn't a pearl, the word. It wasn't made smooth. It became a new word, a word that was sharp. A word as longtooth, knife.

I don't know how any of this was done. I guess I can do tricks too. And if you want to know if this stuff really happened. Like if I am telling it in metaphors. Like what are the facts. And then maybe more generally which of my stories, or which of any story at all, is true. I will say: the one you are reading is true. I will say: get lost, and I will mean it kindly, as invitation to come along.

When my heart was done squeezing itself onto the word

23

what remained was an ugly, barbed thing. It was like the word *cunt*. Or *capitalism*. Of course it wasn't either of those words. It was just something like them. Mostly it was a new word, hollow, ash black. And then: it started to push itself into muscle.

Of course it wasn't her that was stabbing me. It was me. What I had done to the word.

And then: my heart opened up, and my ribs opened up. The ribs felt like dry reeds pushed just to the point where they might splinter but not break. The heart felt like a wound because it was a wound. And the word fell out.

And the word sat wetly on the table.

And the word didn't move. Did I mean it? The word? I did. I didn't. One of my bigger problems.

And my heart felt empty. And I thought: *How cliché*. And I thought: *Well*. And I thought: *Think something smarter*.

I stared at the word and it didn't look right. Something about it being inside me had made it an insufficient vessel. I had taught it a thing or two is what I'm saying. Eventually I started to wonder if I'd really even eaten the right word, if maybe once she got into one word, she was able to swim from one to another. I thought: *Chain of signifiers*.

And then one day I saw her in another word, so I ate that one too. I grabbed it fast and swallowed. It was still alive and wriggling as I felt it make its way through my body. And I knew what I had to do, which was to eat as many words as I could, to gulp down great fistfuls. Which I did. Am doing. Will continue to do until I am stuffed and beyond.

And I took to also eating the rules of language. Where a comma, goes or how you don't start a sentence with and. And that we are supposed to take it serious. That there are ways to be wrong with it.

And then the sounds.

And then the poetry of it too.

I intend to swallow it all, to await its rebirth.

So I can pin her down like an insect on pegboard. So I can see the hollowed-out shapes of her, but really of me.

So that she will be in front of me sitting wetly on the table and I can say I'm sorry or I'm working on it. So that I can eventually find the right.

Right as in correct. Right as in I am entitled to do so.

So that all of this—every word, every drifting memory, every moment—is given my shape, my heritage, finally.

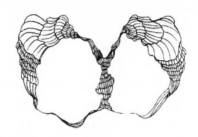

From dusk to dawn, the beast paced a deep furrow in the dirt surrounding the neighborhood. It was a new development. Meaning the neighborhood. The beast had been there a long time, before the gridded-out concrete and cul-de-sacs, before the houses and the human resources representatives that occupied the houses, peering out of their windows into the dark, watching for a flash of furshine in the moonlight.

When the sun came up, the beast left for darker places and everyone went to work. They married and they made children for themselves in daylight. In time they realized that even with no beast they would not have gone out into the dark. In this way, they became civilized. But: this is a love story, not a story about being civilized.

Over time the beast hungered and grew bored. It took to howling at the windows. It mauled a Hyundai Elantra, cutting its gums open on the splintered fiberglass. It hopped fences and shit where it pleased. The beast took to pacing on the concrete of the sidewalks instead of in his furrow. It wandered the streets, ragged now, and empty, and a gently-regarded nuisance instead of what it was supposed to be.

Once, the beast forgot it was a beast. It did not go home at dawn. It ate the food left out for it. It lolled into the lap of a child and nodded off.

Can you believe it? Neither can I. I know a beast. I watched it, with suspicion. I waited for it to be full asleep, past the paw

26

twitch and the lip quiver, until it looked like the rug version of itself. I reached out, then, and I caged it. I caged it in a way that it could never escape, by giving it context and meaning. I caged it in a sentence like this one.

ALI/WENDY

I am upset. I like calling it that: upset. Upset implies that my mood is like a side table that's been knocked over, that things could be righted pretty easily, though most of the time they can't. Most of the time being upset is a sure sign that things have moved into the irrevocable. Take now, for instance, while I sit in Dr. Gary's back office while he says the following thing to my mother and me:

"It would seem that something is very wrong with Alicia's MRI result." He holds up a picture of my brain, which looks like something between packing peanuts and the slime they use to make chicken nuggets. Then he puts it on his desk and slides it over to us, pointing with his ring finger at a darkish spot between two folds, grimacing with a kind of polite deferral that makes it pretty clear he thinks I'm going to die. Mom starts crying.

"What is it?" I ask.

Dr. Gary purses his lips together like a real idiot. "I don't know how to tell you this, Ali."

I look at him and then at my mother, who has covered her face with both hands. It all seems a little melodramatic. I am here because I dove for a soccer ball wrong and clonked myself on the goal frame. I am here for kid stuff, tomgirl stuff. I look at the dark spot that Dr. Gary's finger is still touching. It's not me, because I'm me. I'm here. There's the proof.

Dr. Gary is saying something, has been saying things.

"Have you felt strange lately, Ali? Have you been behaving differently or having unexplainable feelings?"

I know the answer well enough. A week after I lost my virginity, I started having these thoughts that didn't feel like my thoughts. I would be brushing my teeth or running a 5k alongside the other girls on the track team, and it was like the world was about to slide right off of itself, and then it would, and these thoughts would come flooding in. I didn't know what to do about it, so I took a pregnancy test. It turned up negative, but of course my mom found the stick in the trash and came after me. The thoughts kept on, grew louder, more frequent. I could feel myself becoming different from myself. And then the gaps started, where I didn't know what to say, or felt like I was just spectating in my own life. I was in health class at the time, and we were split up by gender and shown slides of genitals in various states of disarray by a visibly nervous tennis coach. I thought what was happening to me was adulthood, some new phase of puberty, at once as normal and as intensely strange as growing breasts.

But I guess it's just a fucking brain tumor.

There's an ant on Dr. Gary's desk, making a wobbly path toward a ring of coffee stain. I reach over and smoosh it with my thumb.

"You've got ants, Dr. Gary."

He frowns. "Ali, I need you to listen to me."

"Ants aren't a very good thing for a doctor's office to have. When we had ants in the bathroom, we set out these traps. They're really cheap, and they work."

"Ali, we're going to have to talk about treatment options."

My mother is still in the room, but also long gone. Dr. Gary looks at me with fatherly worry. He looks nothing like my dad. I want to slap him quite a lot.

Another ant appears from a little crack in the desk and I smoosh that one too and then show Dr. Gary the ant corpse stuck to my thumb. "Ants are really unprofessional."

. . .

The surgery will be Friday. Today is Tuesday. I will be awake through most of it. I'll go under, they'll cut my skull open, and then they'll wake me up while they dig the tumor out. I have to stay awake to help them know if something goes really wrong. They're going to ask me a bunch of questions, and I have to answer, and when my brain goes wonky on them, they know they're going too far.

I picture the tumor like a big booger, and the brain surgeon getting it out of there with a hooked finger. It's a glioma, apparently. I have a pamphlet about it, sitting between me and my mom on the table at Wendy's, partially obscured by our trays. My mom has calmed down some but seems like she might fall off the cliff again at any moment. I'm tired of my Frosty, so I start dipping french fries in it and leaving them there.

"This explains so much," my mom says.

"About what?"

"Your behavior, Ali. Your grades. And, you know..."

I know what she means. "I had sex with Todd because I'm seventeen, Mom, not because of a brain tumor. Everyone in high school has sex, or tries to have sex, or feels bad for not having sex."

"Ali, *voices*," she says. I realize I'm sort of yelling. My mom's lip trembles.

I know what she means about my behavior being the worst part. My grades are garbage this year, but that's because I don't care, and I'm upset a lot. I lost some friends, Maggie and Kelly, but they were lame anyway. I think on what Dr. Gary said about my behavior being maybe odd. I think about maybe only liking Todd because of this thing pressing against my brain. That makes me pretty sad, like, it's the wiring of love stripped bare, and who the hell wants that? I'm supposed to be young, a hopeless romantic, not a bunch of electricity that's buzzing wrong.

I jab another fry into my Frosty. "I'm not different. I'm not special."

What we're not talking about: that a brain tumor likes to come back aggressively if surgery doesn't get it all, that not getting it all means I'm a sad, sad story, and that getting it all and some extra means I'm a different kind of sad, sad story. That I'm going to wake up on Friday with my brain in the open air, and they're going to ask me questions and—just like when I got a prescription for contacts and couldn't tell which was the less blurry choice—I won't know which answer to give, and I'll end up screwing myself.

"Why can't I just be who I am?" I ask my mom, nobody.

She reaches across the table and puts a hand on my wrist. Her eyes are big and wet in her skull. "What do you mean, hon?"

I jerk my hand away. "God, Mom."

She puts her hand over her mouth and squeezes out the tears that have been welling up.

"Sorry," I say. "But it's your *brain* that's sad. What your brain does isn't you. It's structures, pathways, nerves. There's no real meaning to it."

She looks at me like she doesn't get it, even though she was saying the same thing to me by saying I've been different. If the tumor in my brain isn't me, then it stands to reason that the brain itself is not me, and her brain is not her.

I look down at the Frosty cup. The chocolate ice cream byproduct has started melting. There's a little mound of solid in the middle with fries jammed into it and then pooling liquid at the sides. It's oleaginous and slick, either because of the fries or because that's just what a Frosty is. Everything about

31

it is purply-gray like a corpse face.

Wendy smiles up at me from the tray. I clear my fries to the side to see her better. They redesigned her over the summer, and I realize she looks a lot like me. Like, alarmingly like me. Like, those are my freckles, and yeah, my hair is tied back loose right now, but those are my soccer pigtails, and my hair in them, which they made bright red for marketing purposes instead of the orangey-red that I've got, and suddenly I see that it's me selling something to me, and maybe here is where I've been all this time.

I dart my head around to see if anyone notices that I'm Wendy. My mom is still crying. The manager and an employee are looking at us from behind the counter. Those corporate pig-fuckers.

I am standing before I really know it. I march over there and slap my hand down on the counter. "Corporate pig-fuckers!"

"Excuse me?" the employee says, and I realize she's in my civics class, and that's when I really lose it.

Our expulsion from the Wendy's was kind of a brisk blur. My mom tried to explain to them that I'm not myself, but I kept yelling over her that of course I was, and I was Wendy, and a lot of other things that don't make as much sense now that I'm alone in my room. I still think that girl's a pig-fucker.

From my bedroom window, I can watch our chickens scratch around in their coop. There are five hens in all, each of them terribly named by Mom—Cluck Kent, Gregory Peck, Anderson Cooper, Egg Begley Jr., and Henzel Washington. We had a rooster, but he was too much with the crowing, and my mom is the type to consider the neighbors' feelings before the neighbors even consider them.

I get off the bed and dig into my closet. In the corner is a milk crate full of my dad's records, and beneath that is a sagging cardboard box that's seen a few moves. I drag them both out to the bed. Dad's record player is on my desk. He gave it to me before he moved to South America to build an oil rig, plus all his records, plus the junk in the box that's sort of a jumble of the sentimental and the unwanted. The belly-button lint of his life.

I flip through the records. There's a lot of really bad stuff that I put on once and never again. Huey Lewis, Bob Seger— that type of stuff. But there's good stuff too, and I've started to buy some of my own and slip them in. I don't want to listen to any of my stuff, though. All of it's suspect, the tumor's taste instead of my own. I want something of my dad's. I pull out Bruce Springsteen's *Born to Run* and put it on, flick the volume knob as far as it wants to go.

How long has my brain been such an unreliable figure in my life? Is it the tumor that makes it unreliable, or was it always this way? A part of me is able to look at this from a distance, to see that I'm in shock about my situation, that I might die, and now I have to consider all that. And then there's the part of me that has to live through all of it. I get really angry for a minute. And then I get angry that the anger may just be my brain's anger and not mine. And then I get angry at that too.

The harmonica peals over the piano at the beginning of "Thunder Road." I'm in a very complex place. I'm not supposed to like the harmonica, but my dad likes the harmonica. I remember him playing it for me. And I like how aggressively lame Bruce Springsteen was even back then, how he's kind of a dope, and he doesn't even care.

Or maybe I don't. Maybe that's all the tumor. God, it's all so fucked.

The light on my phone is blinking at me. I've been ignoring Todd's texts all afternoon. Bruce and his friends yell out "Whoa—oa, she's the one." I start dancing half-heartedly. I think it might help. I swing my arms around all loose in their sockets. I kick my feet out in front of me. I am dancing like a Muppet or one of the *Peanuts* characters, and it does help, so I do it harder. I feel like a body, like an anything that might happen. Still dancing, I pull things out of the box. There's a little skeleton figurine that collapses when you push the bottom of it. A mesh hat from a truck stop we went to when we were on the trip to Yellowstone. A pocketknife that I remember him using to destroy a beer can when I was very young. A book: a copy of *Player Piano* he thought I would like. I'd always been partial to the Brontë sisters, but I read it anyway. Seeing it now, I hate it some.

I throw the book across the room. I think of a line from *Wuthering Heights* about getting wild. Then: I get wild.

I'm not supposed to drive until way after the surgery, so I'm on my bike, pumping down the road. It's one of those wide-handled fixies from the sixties. I'm sure I look an idiot standing up on the pedals, pushing with all my might up the hill on Parker Road, but I don't care. It's a Wednesday after midnight and I've got a backpack full of eggs plus my dad's pocketknife clipped to my tank top. The knife bangs against my chest like a heartbeat trying to leave a bruise. My body is a tumor is me is an inconsequential thing. The tumor and my body are in a fight. My mom is in an unconsummated fight with my dad since he's unreachable on the oil rig. I'm in a fight with a multinational corporation that has stolen my me without permission. Being alive involves a great deal of strife today.

I feel a lot of things but don't care about any of them. Being upset and being not upset are the exact same I've realized. Part of me thinks I should keep the tumor. I know that's crazy, but again, there's not a distinct difference between something crazy and something sane if thoughts are physical things that happen inside of a space, with sparks or chemicals and the shape of the pathways of the brain coming together to do what they're destined to do. All physical things are equitable and therefore basically meaningless. My bike. The knife at my chest. The eggs in my bag. I don't question the value or truth of these objects. My thoughts are no different.

I am not afraid of anything. I am riding my bike up a hill to the Wendy's. I am not afraid of anything.

When I get to the parking lot, I'm winded, my chest heaving and burning. I let my bike clatter on the pavement. The lights are out inside the restaurant, but the sign is still on. My ghost-lit face glares out at me. My pack pulls me backward as I unshoulder it. I'd gathered up all the eggs from the chickens out back of our house, plus everything that was inside the egg bowl on the kitchen counter. The hens lay like crazy, and there's just me and my mom eating them. It's a lot of eggs.

I unzip the pack and pull out the first gallon storage bag. A few eggs broke on the bottom, but that's okay. I heft one of them in my hand and then let loose with all my intramural softball might. It bursts against the plate glass in a way that's almost beautiful. I let fly with two or three more. Lord, this feels amazing. I turn to the sign over my head and try to smear my beatific, shining face. The first few sail over, but then I bullseye my stupid stolen freckle-face with yolk. Pelting my lit-up self with eggs, I feel enormous. If I could stay in this moment, if there were infinite eggs and my arms didn't tire, if the moon would sit still in the sky and the sun went right to hell—if all of that happened I'd find comfort of a sort. If the only certain thing is that the me in the sign is the me that's down here, then the sign should be as ruined as I am, and it should be frozen forever in that ruining. Maybe then a part of me could get loose and go on.

I have an egg in each hand and more at my feet, and I am flinging with plenty still left to do when the cop shows up. I can't see him for the flashlight he's shining in my face. He tells me to put my hands up, so I do, holding the eggs high.

The cop walks up and points the flashlight at the ground between us. "The hell are you doing, girl?"

He's got his other hand on the butt of his gun. I guess it's like a comfort for him. I know he sees the knife clipped to my shirt. Part of me wants to grab on to it, the way he's touching his gun. I look up at Wendy, smiling all vacant and carefree.

I don't reach for my knife. Instead, I speak for it. I say, "Please don't touch me."

The cop stands firm. "I'm not gonna touch you."

"I just really don't want to be touched right now. If you touch me, I don't know what will happen."

"No one's touching you as long as you cooperate. What's your name?"

"Wendy."

Things get tense with the cop and then he about bursts into tears when he gets my mom on the phone and gets hold

36

of the whole sobby story. I'm not really there for any of it, so I don't know. I hate that cop as much as I hate anybody, though. My mom picks me up and drives me home and then keeps me at the kitchen table a long time. She puts a slice of pie in front of me that I don't eat.

She says, "Ali, it's okay."

I smash pie between the tines of my fork.

She says, "Really, Ali, it's going to be okay."

The pie becomes a kind of pinkish mush the longer I work at it, until it's no longer pie at all. The cop took the knife from me but gave it back to my mom. I don't know what she's done with it, but I want to hold it a minute. I like the fake wood grain, the metal clip that you can pull away far enough to get a pinky under, the solid stiffness of how the blade pivots out from the handle. And maybe if I hold it some of the molecules would trade stuff with some of my molecules. Maybe everything I touch becomes a little bit me, and in this way I will make my escape.

Finally my mom asks, "Why'd you do it, Ali?"

"I'll be dead on Friday."

"Don't say that. That's not true. Dr. Gary says it's in a good spot to get it all."

I look at her like she's stupid. "Dr. Gary has ants, Mom."

"What does that have to do with it?"

"He's an optimist. Out of touch with reality. Not to be trusted."

My mom scrunches up her face like she's holding back from calling me a dope. Well, maybe I'm a dope. I smash my pie more, half-heartedly.

After a second she says, "Okay, but the Wendy's? Surely there'd be something more meaningful to egg than that."

I put my fork under my pie plate and lever it rhythmically.

It rattles my mom's teacup in its saucer. Mom reaches over and takes my plate away. I make a face of mock surprise, and she smiles. I reach for it, and she picks up a fork, pretends to stab my hand. We sit quiet for a minute, feeling comfortable, feeling like nothing terrible is happening.

"Todd called the house," she says. "After dinner. I'm sorry I didn't tell you."

"It's fine."

"I didn't tell him."

I feel my face get hot. "Thank you."

The sky out the window gets a little lighter. We sit here. My mom drinks tea with two-handed sips. Finally I say, "If I don't get to be me, why should a corporation?"

My mom looks at me, confused, a little scared. "What do you mean?"

"They're supposed to be faceless."

My mom is going to cry again. I sort of want her to, so I say, "How could you let all this happen?"

There it is.

I skip school and fall asleep on the couch around noon. I wake hours later to my mom holding a phone out for me, and for a minute I don't know where I am, don't realize it's late afternoon and the sun is starting to sink behind the neighboring houses. I think it must be morning, the way the light looks.

"It's your father," my mom says. She's holding her hand over the receiver. "He's on the rig but talk as long as you want."

I sit up and take the phone. She walks into the kitchen. "Dad?" I ask. I feel like a kid who broke a lamp.

His voice is echo-ey, cuts in and out: "Ali? Ali, are you there?"

I want to say this is a hard question, but the connection is bad, and I don't know what he knows. "I'm here."

"Ali, I'll be there on Saturday morning. It's the soonest I can get a helicopter and a flight back."

"Okay, Dad." I picture him getting on the chopper. I bet they call it that: a chopper. I bet he looks very important, and the roughnecks all gather around in hushed awe as he lifts off, and he watches from the window getting small. I bet someone makes a dark joke about his daughter dying, and I bet the daughter is me.

There's a little delay from the satphone that we're used to from the past few years of birthday phone calls. We have become polite phone-talkers, each waiting to be sure the other one doesn't have something more to say. He says, "How are you handling it?" We wait for my answer.

"I'm fine. I listened to *Born to Run* last night. It made me feel a little okay."

"What? Where'd you get that?"

I look at the pattern on the couch. It's been in the living room since I can remember, this terrible watercolor flower upholstery in greens and blues. Probably it's older than I am. Probably it was here before the house, like they built a living room and then the house and a neighborhood around it after finding the thing in the wilderness.

"Ali?"

"I got it nowhere. I don't remember."

"Ali, it's going to be okay, okay?"

"People keep saying that, yes."

"Ali."

"Dad, I know you love me. I know you're not here because

39

of how you love me, and that you don't know a better way to show it than earning money for my college. You don't have to prove anything in a phone call."

Silence. I realize the line is dead. I hang up, and the phone rings immediately in my hand like an accusation. I answer.

"Ali?"

"Dad."

"I don't know what happened. I lost you."

I find a seam in the couch and stick a finger in, feeling the foam underneath the fabric, and then the wood, and a metal spring. "That's okay, Dad. I think I did too."

There's a longer pause on the line where we both realize we're pretty much fucking this up. Which is typical of us, but he's the parent, so I tend to put it all on him. What do my parents want but comfort from me, and why should I have it to give? A good question if anyone was around to answer. I think about my brain giving birth to Wendy, only to have her do her best to wreck everything. Most metaphors are dumb as hell once you realize they're metaphors.

"Ali?"

"I think I'm in the weeds, Dad." An old saying of his.

"I know, baby."

I can hear his breath, and then I can smell it, cigarettes and decaf coffee, and I know this isn't memory, this smell. It's something else that I'm actually smelling, and I get small and a little afraid.

"I think I'm scared," I say, "but I don't know for sure."

"It's okay to be scared, Ali."

"But what if I don't know if I am?"

I see my mom watching from the doorframe. I turn away from her and whisper into the phone. "I can't be sure of anything. I don't know what's me, and what's not, or what

40

matters about any of it. I mean, Dad, are you you or your brain? And if your brain betrays you, then who's betraying who? I can smell you. I shouldn't, but I can. And that's not me, or it's me. And I don't think there's such a thing as recovering from this."

I realize he's been saying my name for a while now, like: "Ali, Ali, Ali."

"What?"

"I'm going to pack a bag now, and by the time I see you, you'll be sure of everything. And if you're not, I'll make you sure. I don't know how to do most things. You've got your mother for most things. But I can do that."

I know that he's all-the-way wrong. That he sees the world as easy and fixable. An engineer, my dad.

"Okay?" he says.

"Okay."

I spend the rest of the daylight with the chickens. They've got a little wired-off box that takes up about a third of the yard, and if I bring some fruit in there with me they'll gather around, heads bobbing with their emptied-out eyes. One of them, Henzel, is a Plymouth Rock, and the rest are Australorps and Rhode Islands. They're good-looking birds, I guess. I hold out an old strawberry and they peck at it until it falls apart or I drop it.

This is where Todd finds me when he comes around back. He calls my name, and I twist around to see him looming between me and the setting sun, the fingers of one hand looped through the chicken wire. Either the angle of him is playing tricks on me, or he's just getting taller and taller. Already he's six-foot-four. He plays on the high school basketball team, but he's such a lousy shot that he does more harm than good. Everybody likes him, though, because he doesn't seem to care whether the shot goes in or not. He's just happy to hold everyone's attention.

"Where were you today?" he asks.

I squint up at him and shield my eyes from the sun. I can't make him out at all. "Skipped," I say.

"Your mom know?"

"Yeah."

He looks over at the house. One of the chickens hops onto my leg and I shoo it off.

"Ali, what's going on?"

I stand up and brush the grass and chicken feed off my legs. "Go away, Todd."

"Lane Thompson says you flipped out on her last night, that you were screaming all these crazy things."

I shrug. I start leaning back into the coop and then bouncing up off it again. I want this to be not happening. I want to be alone with my chicken friends. I think to myself that if I was dead already I wouldn't have to tell Todd he doesn't matter, or explain to him that nothing matters in the way he thinks it matters. I stand on one foot, then the other.

"What are you doing?"

"I'm sorry," I said, "I'm just trying to stay interested in right now."

Even standing up, I still have trouble making him out because of the sun. I can see the outline of his box shoulders, his hair all sweaty from a run, but I can't see his face or what it's doing. I sort of love it, this lack of information. What his face does is just what his brain makes his face do anyway, and if I hurt his feelings, well, why know about it? It has nothing to do with anything.

"You're being pretty shitty right now," he says.

"Probably."

"Probably?" The question smells like malt vinegar.

"There's no way of knowing for sure."

We both stand there on opposite sides of the wire, and it's another fucking metaphor. "Listen," I say, "this is stupid. Can we jump ahead to the end?"

"The end of what?"

"It doesn't matter of what." I kick at the chickens so they'll move away from the door. I can tell without looking that my mom is watching from the window. "I'm just tired is all. And I've got work to do. So if you want to be around me, you can help me. Otherwise . . ." I make a noise with my mouth like *shwoot* that I use when I'm trying to get the chickens in their coop, and I wave him off. He stands there hurt, and I roll my eyes pretty hard in their sockets. Wires in them go back into my brain and give it information about the world, and right now they're saying that things are very flat in the setting sun. Everything outside of me is nearly without dimension. I feel angry, which of course is different from *being* angry. In one of them, you're sure you're right.

"Like what?" he asks.

"Like what what?"

"Like what work do you have to do?"

I look toward the window. My mother has left the frame. I lean into the fence and lock my fingers in his through the chain link and say, "Corporate sabotage."

Todd agrees to meet me in the Wendy's parking lot after midnight. He agrees to get the spray paint, since he's eighteen and can purchase it legally, and he can fit a ladder in the back

43

of his truck. I told him all of it was vitally important, but not why. He pressed me, but I asked him if he trusted me, and I asked it with a sort of implication that trust might equal oral sex. Which probably won't happen. For all I know, when I wake up I might be gay or a devout Mormon or the new Dalai Lama. The brain takes shape on its own. Still, he agreed, and I got to keep my mouth shut about everything going on with me.

When I sneak down the stairs, I find my mom waiting for me in the kitchen, drinking tea in the dim glow of the light over the stove.

"Ali, you're not going out tonight."

"What are you doing up?"

"You'd probably call it fulfilling a biological imperative, but I'm being your mother."

"I don't need a mother."

"Well you've got one."

I stand in front of her and wait. I think if I wait enough she'll dissipate right in front of me along with the rest of the house. I wiggle the fingers on one hand at my side.

My mom says, "I'm scared too, you know."

"I know."

She looks where I'm looking, which is the door.

"You're going to the Wendy's?"

I nod.

"Because you think they stole your face."

I can feel the anger in my throat and shoulders.

She says, "I'm just trying to understand, Ali."

I think I'm going to yell, but instead I start crying. "They stole my whole me, Mom."

She gets up and wraps me up in a hug. I stand there rod-straight and try not to let her comfort me, but because the comfort is all electrochemical it works a little no matter what.

She's saying *ohhoneyohhoney*, and I know it's prayer, so I say it too. I feel a muted kind of better.

She lets go and steps back, grabs on to my shoulders. Then she brings me in again. "I'll drive you."

We get in the minivan without further comment. Mom drives up the hill, turns on to Main without a blinker. As we approach the parking lot, she dims the headlights. I know she's crying, but I don't look at her. I know that if I look at her I won't be able to be me. I'll be Wendy, or my brain, or the tumor, or something. I'll be someone who doesn't feel so upset, and I don't want that. I want to be me for a minute.

Todd is sitting, his long legs on the concrete, leaning against the building with a shopping bag next to him. When he sees my mom in the van, he stands up awkwardly and looks around, like *Should I be here?* My mom waves.

I get out of the van and walk over to him, point toward the bag. "Thank you."

He shrugs. I bend down and get the bag. There are two cans of black spray paint in it, just like I asked. I pull one out and start shaking it.

"What's your mom doing here?" Todd asks.

"Chaperoning."

"And what am I doing here?"

"You're helping me deface that," I say, pointing up to the sign. "Or unface it. I want it face-free."

He looks up at it. "Why?"

I want to punch him very hard in the sternum, but instead I say, "Did you get the ladder?"

"It's in my truck."

"Well go get it."

He walks off, and I look back at the minivan. My mom

gives me a limp smile. I don't know her right now. I don't know if this is something I'm going to eat shit for or not. I guess if I live long enough, I will, and this will become funny in a bittersweet way. We're not there yet, but I'd like to get there. From where I'm standing I miss her. She might as well be on the moon. Everything is thoroughly upset.

Todd comes back with the ladder and sets it up by the sign. It's tall but maybe not tall enough. I rattle the paint more and start to climb. On the second step I stop and put a hand on Todd's shoulder, taller than him finally.

"Thank you," I say, "but go home now."

"This is my dad's ladder." The worry on his face is simple, clear, and about the ladder. I know this is the last time we'll hang out, whether or not I'm still me tomorrow, whatever me is.

"We'll bring it back in the van."

He scowls.

"I promise. You don't want to get in trouble for this, and you won't if you go home."

He slinks off to his car without saying anything else. I don't bother watching him pull away. I climb the ladder.

At the top, I shake up a can and begin. I spray paint on close and thick so it kills the glow of the sign. The paint drips down over my face as I blot out the hair, the brow, the eyes. At a certain point, I realize my mom is holding the ladder. The black is glossy, slick. It covers over the light even as it gathers up new light and reflects it outward. It's not the light from some distant star. It's just light from the parking lot. Still, it feels good to make something blank, to see what blankness offers up. Her face is gone, replaced by a sloppy, dripping rectangle. And that's it.

I expect something else to happen. Relief, epiphany,

something. But it's just me and my brain up here, intertwined and spiraling toward something—just like before. The urgency I felt drains out of me, leaving behind something sheepish and real. I look down at my mom. She's looking up at me. I set the can on the top of the ladder.

"What comes next?" she asks.

"That's it," I say. "We go home."

I wake in the blue room. They're asking and asking and I must be open now. I say I'm cold and they say their say. And the asking. And the light. And the prions and neurons and the *I'm energy and flow*. And the passing back and forth of me, cell to cell, shape to shape, word to word to word to word to word, is a kind of me. And the other kinds of me: the body, the committee, the memory, the stain of me on others, their question again, the answer they want. And the glow behind my face shining back at me in a parking lot is in this room, and the blackness that covers the glow, that keeps it from the world, is in this room, too, in every room forever I'll bet. And the *who I am now*. And the *each*, the *all*. And the *I'm me*. And the *it's me*. And the *I think it's me*.

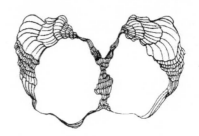

The next village came and stole our baby, our only one. Now we aren't village but hunting party, kitted out in flannel, with sharp sticks, with baby-catching nets and the blood of a lamb on each of our faces. The mother comes forward and puts her hands in the lamb's open guts and smears blood on her own face, takes up her own stick, and we go.

We go into the woods and not all of us come out the other side. The vines of the wild thin us, hunger and cold and infection. Others turn back in disgust, missing Hulu Plus, missing cell phone service. One is made beast and we have to do what we do to beasts. We agree we'll leave that out of the story. We'll leave it in the dark before the triumph to come.

At the edge of the wood, the mother smudges us with sage. She presses her lips to our foreheads. It's not a kiss but an imprinting. Somewhere along the way we became her children, and we march through the plains surrounding her the way a nest might to warm a bird.

We arrive at the next village early in the morning. Automatic sprinklers are running. A garbage truck blunders around gathering up trash. It is a peace like the peace we had. The mother comes forward, then, and screams, and in that scream is a splinter of human suffering unlike and also exactly like any other.

We set on the village, house to house. For the baby we set pets loose and hurl stones to brain them running. For the baby *we light fire to the garbage and the apricot trees. For the baby we slit all throats. We chase them all down, we tine them to the ground with pitchforks, we kill them in their beds and on their toilets and at their kitchen tables, we tackle and twist and tear. All this ugly to honor a child.*

We find it, gasping and furred with its tail wrapped around its throat. We cannot pry the tail free. Everything we try seems to twist it tighter. We bring the mother, and she holds it to her bared breast as its lips go blue, as it tries to cry and can't. She holds it as it goes still. We stand there, watching, silent and victorious.

ALLIES

In the morning, there's a body in the pocket-size park off 5th Street. The body is facedown, one arm bent back and one thrown out to the side, legs crossed over one another like a fall is what killed the body, but it wasn't a fall. There's blood to tell us otherwise, and the back of the body's head to tell us otherwise, hit with something hard by someone strong. The body is attended by the statue in the park of a chimpanzee, Washoe, the first to communicate in sign language, and here above the body the statue signs also with its bronze hands: *friend.*

We are a small town with a college. We loved the college, which kept mostly to the north side and a few of the bars. We loved the sense of connection to the larger world that the college brought. We didn't attend the plays on campus, and we didn't visit the art exhibits, but we liked knowing that they were there. The body belonged to that college—it must have, as the college drew students from all over our state to this place. This safe place.

This is a place where a woman might spin her baby around in a dark alley, where the restaurants all close at nine. This is a place with a farmer's market and Patagonia jackets, a place nestled by hills and known for its wind, the way it might blow your sign away, the extent of our frustrations ending there, or in a neighbor's yellowed lawn, or in the sad, flatulent tuba practice of the boy on his porch, or in winter lasting a few weeks too long. We were a progressive kind of rural, homey. We did not ask for a body. We were not the place to have one. This is not who we are. Here we are.

Of course the body is a black body. You knew that already. The woman who first saw the body, Grace Kapnick, was out walking her dog Keeks. The sun had just crested the hills, and this was the first week of icy sidewalks. Keeks was a Yorkie. Grace was up before the city put down any salt. She had the shoes for it, but she had to go slow while Keeks pranced in his bewilderment, sniffing everything's hard new scent. When she reached the park, which really was just a few hundred square feet of nicer brickwork and potted shrubs nestled between a bank and an alley and then the old movie theater that had become a church, she wasn't looking. It was Keeks who noticed. A dog is a dog, after all.

Grace's breath caught when she finally realized what Keeks was stretching leash over. The blood had frozen to the decorative brick. The ice crystals forming on its surface had begun to pink it. Washoe was wearing a cheapy Santa hat. We were always finding ways to dress him. He was our friend.

Teddy was the first officer on the scene. He sucked on his teeth, radioed for the University police to come down. The two departments had a cordial relationship. They spent most of their time chasing meth and property crime. Occasionally, a rape, but they didn't much share beers over that. Teddy liked his job. It made him feel like a good guy. Really.

Teddy took one look at the body, though, and knew he was in a new kind of trouble. He stood there in the shadow of the theater church, in a yellowing dawn, while other police blocked off the alleyway and the intersection on either side of 5th St. Teddy heard the sound of ripping packing tape—the officer up the street was stripping the farmer's market sign that was still taped to the barricade. Teddy wanted a cigarette. His daughter had made him quit years ago.

When the campus police arrived, they didn't want the body. Neither did Teddy or Teddy's boss. It was as though the refusal would make the body go away, but the body just lay there without claimant, its face frozen stuck to the ground by its own blood. Photos were taken, no wallet found. No hat or jacket, either. From the twist of the body's arms, Teddy assumed that the jacket was taken. Perhaps the hat was knocked off when the blow was struck, but Teddy and the campus police couldn't find it.

Meanwhile, the rest of us were all arising and getting ready for the day. Soon we would ask what the body meant, and the lack of claiming, what it meant, too, and if the police departments didn't want the body because it was a body or if they didn't want it because it was a black body. No one had woken yet who might consider the body a boy, a Derrick, which it was.

The news spread up and down blocks as we woke. South to the coffee shop, north to campus. The street was cordoned off entirely, as was the alleyway. The pastor of the church that used to be a movie theater was barred from entering, since his office overlooked the crime scene, and he was the one who first brought the news to us. *There's a body in Friendship Park.* We sat in our disbelief, holding unsipped lattes. We had shopped so local. We had flown our rainbow flags. We had stickered our bumpers and loved our neighbors as long as they kept scrap metal out of their front yard. Plainly: we were bumblefucked by how we got to here.

In the children's room of the library, Sarah told her reading group that something bad had happened, but that they were safe, and the police would protect them, and to look for the good in hard moments. A young girl fiddled with the hem of her dancer's outfit, thinking of later, when she would get to be a mouse in the children's production of *The Nutcracker*.

The woman who owned the record store sat outside it

smoking a clove cigarette. People walking by regarded her the way they might a panhandler.

A man in no shirt yelled *I'm gonna rap your ass raw* from his back porch while his son climbed too far up the branches of an old and rotting elm.

Two high school kids went by on longboards, blowing sweet-smelling vapor as they went, hooliganing but not really hooligans.

All over town, people were alive.

In his home office, the president of the university got a phone call about the body and then began drafting an email to the students. When he wrote these emails, his body would be wracked—it took physical effort, a tensing of the shoulders and seizing of the breath, to write something that he knew would be, at best, cold comfort. In these moments he felt old, which he was. Keys clacked, taking him further away from the students he sometimes wanted to know how to love.

The body sat on the ground through midmorning while more photographs were taken. A smattering of people watched from each barricade, unable to see around the corner of the building into the park itself. Everyone around town said that it was a shame. The general consensus was that the body had *happened* to us, as bodies had happened to so many communities in the nation. We called it *recent troubles*. We called it *a symptom of the national mood*. It being the body, the body being the black body, the black body being a boy. We did not dare drill down to the bare and ugly truth like that though. We did not think of how one of us had held a baseball bat, or held a brick in their hand, or held something else, we didn't know what, we didn't want to know what, and all of this was such a shame.

On campus, an effort was made, both officially and

unofficially, to see who was missing. Teachers checked their rosters. Students texted their absent roommates. The Office of Student Success jackknifed from one plan to another without succeeding at much of anything. Were the students all accounted for? There was no telling. Many of the kids spent their weekends elsewhere.

The body went to the county coroner's office nameless. The park's dirt was swept up into evidence bags. The Santa hat, too. The shrubbery was poked and prodded thoroughly. By early evening, a man from the city came with a pressure washer, gave Teddy a cigarette. The sun was plunging beyond the hills earlier every day, and Teddy watched and smoked while the man sprayed the brick in the oncoming dark. Neither of them noticed the way Washoe was misted with blood, his bronze skin mottled already by time and caught in evening light.

That night, Keeks ran without warning into the kitchen and came back with a bloody mouse struggling in his jaws. He shook it, and he shook it. It wouldn't die. Grace had to bring a heavy book down on it.

We all got very drunk. Big Tom came into the bar wearing his coveralls and cracking jokes about neglecting his wife. He could never read the mood. When we told him what had happened, he pulled off his hat, showing his balding head with wisps of hair in every direction, everything about him seeming suddenly saggier than it had been. It was a bad night.

At around one in the morning, Teddy stepped out the back door of a bar and vomited into the alley. His wife knew enough not to text him her worry. The town was too small and boring for cheating, and he always walked to the bar when he felt a drunk night coming on. Still, looking at his phone he wished she'd sent him a little something, or that she'd rubbed his back a little before sitting down to dinner. Just something.

He wiped his mouth and lit the cigarette he'd borrowed. His jacket was inside, hung on a hook under the bar. He left it and started walking up the alley, smoking and shivering as he went. He cut over one alleyway so he would pass the park. He couldn't think of a reason why not, and he wanted to see it again, maybe to assure himself that it was still there at all. Some drunk thinking like that.

This is how he came to find Washoe draped in an olive track jacket, a beanie on his head. He flicked his cigarette into the street and jogged over, furious and dumb-drunk. The beanie was black, and he pulled it off the chimp's head and held it up to the streetlight. It was stained, a barely visible brown dully shining in the knit.

Terry stared at the blood. His lips and the top of his cheeks tingled from drink. He rubbed it, the blood. It was dried into the fabric, and it felt a little stiff when he ran his thumb across it. He didn't want to think about any of this. He didn't want to think about what it meant to dress Washoe with the dead body's clothes, or to deal with the way his mind got all knotted up when he tried to reckon with an evil like this living in a place so gorgeous and mundane. That evil isn't mystic. That it's small, and petty, and isn't some force in the world that propels people to do ill but the result of that ill freely being done.

More than anything he wanted to be in bed with his wife, the way they used to get all tangled up and foolish with each other. God, just the smell of her shoulder at night. It carried him through. When we saw Teddy most mornings and asked him how he was doing he'd say *Man, the world's pretty good, right?* And he'd slap our backs as he walked by.

He didn't ever speak on that night, at least not to any of us. He did what he did, maybe because he thought it would save us, or maybe because he couldn't believe it—that this was his town—and he felt he was being cheated by the mockery of it all.

Had we known his reason—if he would have just tried to explain—we might have forgiven him, but: he took the jacket and slid his arms into it. He slipped the beanie in a pocket. He walked on home and stuffed both beanie and jacket in the trash outside his back door. He walked into the house and on to the dark of the bedroom.

Later, when he lost his job, it became another part of what the body had done to our town, losing such a steadygoing part of the community. We couldn't imagine a time when he would stay in his house with the blinds drawn, and then, without ceremony, move over the mountains. But all of that was still on the way.

The next morning, we wanted to breathe easier. The body was still in the county but not in our town. Still, Grace found herself taking Keeks up a block instead of going by her usual route, which meant she would walk by the Planned Parenthood and the Ford dealership to avoid seeing Washoe. The fence of the auto lot had been plastered with enlarged photos of angelic babies, their peach skin seeming to hold all the sunlight, imploring by their very presence opposite the clinic. Grace loved seeing those babies. Her daughter was grown, her little Squish all alive and limby now and out there in the world, wearing a pencil skirt on the west side of the state.

The pastor of the movie theater church made a show of being troubled. On campus, the students clustered together in the student union. Big Tom woke up alone and feeling wounded while sunlight splayed all over the room. Teddy called in sick to work. We were all unsure of ourselves in one way or another. A news van from the city stuck around.

Days went by. The body's people were found. The parents lived in the suburbs of the city over the mountain, in a place where childhoods were good and uncomplicated. They didn't come, but an aunt did. She arrived red eyed and looking tired. When someone asked her how she was she said *How do you think I am* and we all clenched in embarrassment. We told her we were preparing a vigil, which was true. City leaders had been planning it all week. She seemed less than impressed. We kept and kept and kept forgetting her name.

The vigil was held at the fairgrounds. The mayor spoke, flanked by campus and town officials. So much of the town came out to see, to hold candles that were left from last year's Easter service. The mayor rebuked. The president of the university pounded the podium and said that this was not us, and he turned his words toward the goodness inside each of us, and we believed him. We held signs and cheered. We put our children on our shoulders while our dogs scrapped with each other and tangled leashes. We exhaled and watched our breath disappear into the dusk as the air turned crisp. We lived in the shadow of great mountains, and the snow was headed here to snug us away indoors. The mountain pass would close, and we would bear it gladly, our isolation from the world. The hot cocoa of it all. Though this was a hard time, we felt in that moment that we would find it again, and soon. We looked on one another, glad that this was us. We started to feel something like assuaged.

The aunt came forward.

When she spoke, it was with a small voice, but one filled with shattering, tremulous anger. She called us cowards and fools. She accused each of us of being complicit. She said that this is what white folks do, and that we'd been doing it for long enough that there was nothing else left to define us. She said other things we don't care to think about. She told of the time she'd sat the boy down and told him to look out, that something was coming for him and he should be ready, that his parents were fools for letting him ever come to a place like this. She said she'd made sure he was ready, but we came anyway. We snatched him right away. We bodied him.

Later, we would find ways to forgive her, to say that this was not what she meant, that she was blind in her grief and saw us as enemies instead of as who we really were. Later, there would be time for salve. But there, in that moment, we were laid bare by her rage and we hated her more than we'd ever hated anything, and that's what was true in each of us.

We don't know where the first rock came from. We don't know, except that it came from the crowd, that it came with purpose, and that it struck her square in the chest, causing her to step back. Another sailed beyond her, plonging off the flagpole behind. A third bounced from the posterboard sign that a college student had made that proclaimed *love will win*. More rocks followed, more than could be accounted for, more than we thought might be found in the grassy muck of the fairgrounds. Certainly more than could come from our hands. Certainly there was some outside force—history, maybe, or the devil loosed in America. Some of them struck true, and some didn't, and the aunt in her cringing seemed to only become more deserving of welts, of the pain there was to give, of something striking the soft frail parts of her and doing harm. The rocks, they came, and though we would later speak on it like they sprung entire from some other force than what we had in us, there was the weight of them in our hands and the flinging and the gentle spin given by fingertips and the roughness and the chalky residue of rock dirt and the boy of six who threw one straight up in a parabolic arc, glee on his face, that glee we pretend is alien, but is wholly our own.

The aunt was hurried to a car, her head down, leaving us there in our not-yet shame. And that was that.

The question of who made it a body stayed unanswered. The body stayed dead. I want to tell you that we learned his name, or that we learned his father built airplane engines in the city, or we learned that his mother would come across an old t-shirt in the basement still with the funk of boysweat lingering on it and know fully as she folded it back and tucked it neatly into its box that this would be her life, this always reaching for what's not there, and that no amount of our being good would make that not what was true for her now. I want to tell you I didn't kill that boy and leave him there erased just so I could tell the story in a way that made me feel better, that made me feel like I'd done something real about it for once. I want to tell you that not all of this is about me. I want to tell you that I'm an ally, and I want that to mean something, and I want you to believe me.

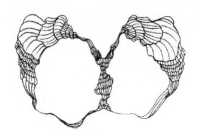

The squid grappled with the shark in the deepest part of the deep, and in this way the world kept going. It had been years of this, though sharks don't know years, and squid don't know the shift and sway of the sun overhead, making their life as they do in different types of blue. Squid believe themselves eternal.

The shark was only hungry. It had grown so lean twisting and thrashing past tentacles. Its jaws working. Its gills constricting and then gasping back open. Its eyes rolled over white for fear of a beak. A shark that goes blind is no longer even a shark, which sharks know.

The squid, for its part, felt dissatisfied with life. How long could it fend off teeth, and why was that supposed to be enough? The squid felt listlessness gathering in the shark's scraping skin. It squeezed harder, wrapped itself around and away from the sharpest parts of a shark, and the shark sagged, saddened, a loosening spring. The squid thought to let go. The squid thought there might be a way to be gentle and squid at once. But when it slackened and started to drift, the shark whipped around again, anew anew.

Have you been in the deep? It goes on and on, and there's hardly anything there even if you know how to look. It's a place where a question might have the grace to go unasked, where it might stay kind.

SCAB

There was a brown spot on the wall. It looked a little raised, but that could've been an illusion created by the combination of the color and the wall's texturing. My thinking was it was a bug, and then, when I got up closer, some kind of bug residue. Maybe an egg sac. My thinking mostly was: gross. That's gross.

I come from a long line of amateur household investigators. My strongest memory of my mother is her bent over in the living room, her nose inches away from the carpet, saying, "What is that?" And of course picking it up, bringing it over to show us kids, saying, "Do either of you know what this is?" Invariably, it was a piece of goldfish cracker or chocolate, but one time it was an actual mouse turd there in her hand.

Later she vacuumed herself into a corner and wept until I got home from school. Things had gotten worse by then, but like it or not, I was still her daughter.

The point is: I picked at it with my finger. And when I picked it, it came loose at one end, and underneath was an angry, pink spot that started leaking a clear and yellowish fluid.

It was a scab. It was a scab on the wall in the house I lived in, in the world I lived in, next to the room I sleep in, and things sort of opened up inside of me so that I felt a little sick.

I let the crust of it fall to the floor. I left the room. I came back. The spot was shining in its moisture, a bead of some liquid gathering at the bottom of it, ready to slide down the wall. I did not want it to slide down the wall. It began to slide down the wall. I left the room. I came back.

This went on for a time. Eventually I phoned in to work,

then gathered myself and called an exterminator, eyes still locked on the leaking space on my wall.

A voice on the phone said *Hello*. It sounded like my father.

"I have an infestation," I said.

What kind?

I stood there, unable to say to him *skin, scab, unreality.* These are not things you say to a man who sounds like your father. Finally, I said, "I'm not sure, but something has damaged my wall."

A man came. I don't think the same man. He smelled strongly of burrito, had a lot of hair on his arms running right up into his shirtsleeves. I led him over to the spot on my wall. He leaned in and looked at it. It had scabbed over fresh, bright pink and enflamed. And: it had grown. What had been the size of the end of my pinky was now the size of a penny.

"What is it?" I asked

He put his face against the wall, trying to see around the edges of it. "Dunno," he said.

He pulled a knife from his belt and flicked the blade open with one finger. "Don't worry," he said, "I'm not gonna hurt your wall." I believed him well enough. He had a kind of working-class authority that came from the eradication of small lives. But when he pressed the blade against and then into the scab, a spray of blood burst forth, spritzing him across the cheek and neck. He jerked back and wiped it away with the back of his blade hand. I saw he was scared, which made me more scared. He backed away from the wall and me both.

"Lady," he said, "what the hell is going on here?"

I tried to make my voice as small as I could when I said, "Please just help me."

He was staring at his hand still. "Fuck you, lady."

And he left me there. He stormed right on out. I imagine he was more afraid than angry, but I still felt like I owed him an apology. I had a habit of apologizing for things that weren't my fault. If it was happening and I was there, I was ready to assume the mantle of blame. I knew it was not the healthiest habit in the world from a mental wellness perspective. I did it anyway.

When he shut the door behind him, I sat on my carpet for a while. There were flecks of blood on it. I moved my hand away, then felt I was being silly, and I put my hand back where it was. I reminded myself that everything can be reckoned with in this world. Then I reminded myself again. I could be scared and reasonable, both at once.

My wall was bleeding still. There was no other way about it: I went to the bathroom and found the first aid kit, stanched the blood with gauze, and bandaged it as best I could. When I was done, I said, "All better." I felt embarrassed, because I realized I may not have been talking to myself and looked around the room.

I made dinner, box macaroni. I tried watching TV. I wasn't successful until I rearranged the furniture in my living room to be facing away from the injured wall. Around nine I had to change the bandage. When I took the old bandage off, rust-red and damp, it had weight. The wound had heat coming off of it. This is normal, I thought. All of this is normal, and everything will be well again soon. I pressed a new bandage to the wall, secured it with medical tape.

When I felt the room breathing, I knew it was my imagination. That almost made it worse. Because: what would I imagine next? The air around me seemed to draw into somewhere and then fill the space again. I thought maybe this is how it started with Mom. One unreasonable thing. One thing beyond controlling. Then she was on her way.

It took three gin and tonics before I could go to sleep. I felt ill drinking them in the kitchen, and I felt ill having drunk them in the bedroom. My hands smelled of squeezed lime while I lay in bed, swimming in the sheets and my drunkenness.

This probably happens all the time, I thought. *It's just new to you.* On my phone in bed, thoroughly drunk, I searched for it, but all I found was noise. I tried different combinations of *scab* and *wall* and *blood* and *wound*. I didn't know what search term would give me an answer. It seemed like there was too much possibility, that I wouldn't find my problem in the realm of all possible problems.

I fell asleep searching.

In the morning, the bandage had fallen and the wound was the size of a peach. It made me jump back when I saw, jerked me right awake. My head throbbed, and I thought: pinky, penny, peach. I tried to think of the next biggest thing that would fit this pattern, if it was a pattern, if it was just my need for a pattern, if there was a difference. Pumpkin. Profiterole. How big are those? Paul Rudd. Pennsylvania.

I had to get things under control, first of all myself. I bit my lip to keep from saying *What's wrong?* I was afraid of who I would be asking, afraid there might be an answer.

I went outside and stood on my lawn, looking back toward my open door. It was a normal Tuesday. An automatic sprinkler was going, and when it reached the end of its arc, it went suddenly deep and full against a city garbage can that had been left out from Monday morning. I thought of my HOA. I thought of Brad Planck's dog shitting in my yard. The world went about its morningish business. I could tell myself I didn't know why it was a relief, to be out here and to see that my door led to the same place it always had, that the grass on my lawn still needed more attention than I was willing to give it. My neighbor across the street was loading his kids into a van like they were cargo, lifting them up and placing them in one by one. He'd come across the pavement once and offered to mow my lawn and I'd said *No, no*. I knew what he thought of me, living alone, a little too old for it in his eyes, a little too single, maybe a lesbian, but not the neighborly kind—the kind of lesbian who is not into yardwork.

He probably owned spackle.

I jogged across the street, waving my arms a little too wildly. His head was ducked into the van, and he was futzing with somebody's seatbelt. His children were totally indistinct to me, just the one and then a smaller one and another slightly smaller one. They had very wispy hair and seemed perpetually syrup-smeared.

"Hey," I called out. We didn't know each other's names, but he smiled at me. "Hey, do you have spackle, or like something to fix a wall?"

One of his kids yelled in the car and he startled and turned before answering. "Yeah, somewhere. You knock a hole in it or something?"

"Something."

"How big?"

I held up my hand, made a circle with two fingers that was a good bit smaller than the wound itself. I didn't want him coming over to take a look. "About yea big."

"I got you," he said. Then he went into his garage and dug around in a drawer for a minute. I stood there not looking at his children while they looked at me. The father came back and handed me a little plastic jar. "That should work, but it might not look as good as a real wall patch."

"It's fine. Thank you. I'll bring it by later."

"Keep it," he said.

I thanked him again, then walked back to my yard. I hesitated at the door, which had swung closed on its own. Had that happened before? It had. I put my hand on the wood and pushed. It was warm from the morning sun.

Inside, the scab was crusted over again, yellow at the edges, then red, shiny and tacky looking still. I thought I might blow on it. I put my hand on the wall, expecting warmth, but got only the cold of room temperature, which always seems colder when you touch something solid than when you're standing in the air.

I went and got a cloth and a butter knife, which was the closest I had to the right tool for the job. The spackle smelled like a new room, one that had never had people in it. I mixed it up with the butter knife. I spread a little on the wall away from the wound, dragged the knife across the wall to smooth it over. It worked well enough. With a fresh coat of paint it might not be noticeable at all, or else it would just be a smooth spot.

I stood in front of the wound, waiting for it to object. I realized I thought of it as a conscious thing, as though it might have a will and a preference for what happens next.

"I have to do this," I said. "You understand."

But of course it didn't understand.

I slopped the spackle onto the wall and pulled down across the wound as gently as I could. When it wouldn't spread, when it got stuck on the ridges of the scab, I spread on more. When it started going pink, when it started having flecks of dried blood mixed in, I started to weep. I put more spackle on. I spread it thick over everything, the whole jar up on the wall. It kept sliding off the wound, sticking to the dry

66

parts. The wall bled freely. I cried more.

"You can't do this to me," I said. The wound was surrounded by globules of spackle. Part of the scab was peeled back and barely hanging. I took the cloth I'd brought with me and dabbed it, watched the blood seep out of the pink flesh of the wall, the way it seemed to come from nowhere and everywhere, a magic trick of the body of my house. Whatever this was, I was going to have to live with it. I sank to the floor.

I sprawled out on the carpet haphazard like a corpse.

I tried to think about meaning.

Like: was this sudden impetus toward caretaking a cosmic corrective for my lack of desire for motherhood, my inability to have attachments? Was it brought on by my neighbor's belief and therefore society's belief that I was somehow lacking without being needed by something?

Like: is this about the environment, the metaphysics of space, and what makes a room a room, and how a room is already a kind of wound?

Like: what even are the suburbs but a betweening of the world of human and animal, and why should I expect one or the other to have dominion?

Like: what makes this less acceptable than any of the other events that happen to me every day?

Like: Breathing.

Like: Having a thought at all.

Like: Being a being that exists at this scale in the context of the infinite.

I decided, finally, that it was meaningless, a fucking up of normal, and I had only to bear it, as I'd borne so many things.

This decision did not make things easier. In fact they got much worse, as I learned to bear more and more things for less and less reason.

Which brings us, quietly, to now.

THE FATHER MAKES A MISTAKE

I know the knife is going to enter my child when I feel time slow. I know there will be an accident. The spatula slipping a little under the cutting board, the placing of the pan down on the pot holder, the levering of the spatula, the launching of the blade, Japanese-make, little dimples in the steel, loosed by the dumb circumstance of the world that got all of us to right here.

Time does not slow enough. *Enough* would be for time to end, for the knife to be unmade by the air it carves. The body I'm in reaches wildly for the knife, making contact with the handle, spinning the blade erratic. The child toddles, the child is looking up toward me, a look of thorough joy on his face. This is a child that doesn't see the wound coming. My child, with a hand out to balance himself on my leg.

There is nothing at all profound about any of this. In many ways a knifeslip is just being alive. In the moment and after, I think of my father, and then of the separate man who raised me, and how one and then the other were not enough to keep me from this. My father the pastor in mid-collapse in front of us, the guttering lawnmower ending its noise just as my brother and I look up from our place there playing in the dirt, the stroke revealing one way a father fails. I learned another from the man who raised me, a man my mother found endlessly forgivable who yet had a meanness that seemed to come from a different person entirely when it came. Wisdom to give, a belt to give it with. I am neither of those men. I am this one.

The knife opens my boy at the shoulder and clatters away. The boy's face makes a new kind of face as I am reaching down for him and all his red. He screams. The scream is an ending. Nothing I do will close the wound. I press him to me. His warmth spreads down my shirt. We are both of us clinging, as if in the clinging we might be saved.

I say, "There's been an accident." I am telling the child to make it in the past, to make the accident not what is present. The child understands time but the wound has its own kind of time and there is so much of the wound. It is all over both of us now.

I press a kitchen towel hard against the open place. The child screams at me to stop. I press him closed again. I keep him as whole as I can. I walk him to the front door and, with the hand that supports his weight, I turn the knob and we are in the yard now. And I am pressing. And I won't fail. And he is screaming into the early autumn night. And we are waiting for what comes next, father and child. We are waiting for what will save us, the sun behind the trees burning across everything. One last moment, gold and pink.

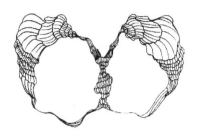

The two kept their knives sheathed, mostly, but that didn't stop the threat of them. One of them had a brass button where one eye should be, and one had a beard angling and tufting out of his several faces. One of them had a Gila monster's severed head for a heart, and one of them ate grass when he could find it, and one of them killed my father with garden shears, and that's why I'm here in front of them.

They weren't men so much as the idea of men. They kept shifting while we waited for the next thing to happen. Parts and pieces is what they were, and the parts and pieces would change wherever it was on them you weren't looking. What was true about one of them might be gone before he even knew it was true his own self. When I say this, I'm saying how it felt, not how it was. How it was was a much more everyday ugly.

I had them cornered in a basement out west. I'd chased them near a year. They might have been my kin, but I didn't know. They might have found redemption along the way. I didn't ask. They might not have needed to die in that basement. One of them, his arm turned to three snakes. I didn't trust it, so I undid it. I kept undoing things about them. I undid them all the way. I said the violence was for my father, but I didn't even know what was true, and I didn't care.

After I was done, I drove home. I turned the radio up, and I rolled the windows, and it was raining, and the rain made me flinch and stung my eyes, and I didn't care.

71

In a field back east I saw them, both of them, wandering out and away from me to do some good or some ill. A deed at any rate. I let it happen, because I didn't care. I watched them go over the horizon. What if I were calm. What if I could be unburdened by my own shifting form.

WHO WE USED TO BE

At night our skeletons chatted while we did our oblivious sleep. We didn't know it was happening. All we knew were aching jaws and tooth pain. Our skeletons couldn't operate our lungs or vocal cords, so they developed their own teeth-clacking code.

A lot of this is still conjecture. A lot of this is just stuff we pass back and forth to kill time in bed, after what we mushily call the jailbreak, while we lay formless under the covers. There's time now for noticing and questions. Questions like: what did they have to talk about? Like: when did they start plotting against us? When did they decide to run away together?

We miss them dearly, our skeletons. That's not conjecture. We're sorry for whatever we did. We puzzle over it all, like it's a mystery that might ever be solved, like there's a way to make our lives become something else entirely if we could just arrive at it and slop the words out of our mouths. But we don't find it. Our lives remain bisected: before and after.

When it first started, we got up each morning alarmed by our sore jaws. "We're so stressed," she said. "We're clenching." But I didn't feel stressed, not really, and neither did she. We were happy in our jobs, in our little home. She made a joke about somnambulism and oral sex. Nobody laughed.

I tried sleeping with a mouthguard, but I would wake up to it between us in the bed, spittle dried on the sheets. She looked at it the third morning, made a face, and said, "Do it or don't, boy." I gave it up.

Did our skeletons love each other because we loved each

other? Were they talking through that love at night, or was it conversation of convenience, prison movie bunk bed stuff? Did they hate us, or were we just in the way? I tell her that I think my heart has moved from its normal place, each beat a bunny hop further to one side of me. She flops her hand periodically toward her long-dead cell phone. We both know she won't ever get to it, let alone plug it back in.

What scares me most is that they might have been right to leave us behind. The cliché of it is that we were spineless already. Instead of a career, we had jobs. Instead of a baby, we got a dog. We fucked infrequently and in the bedroom. We liked nothing better than staying in to watch a movie we'd already seen. We didn't see any of this about ourselves in the moment, but now, in trying to figure out why they might have abandoned us, it's all laid out pretty clearly. Sometimes we think that given the opportunity, we would have shucked free of ourselves too.

It was the dog, actually, who first cottoned to the chattering. He was our precious pup, and when we got him, we spoiled him the way first-time dog owners do. Treats and more treats. Up on all the furniture. He was a distraction and a point of contact for us and just a damn fine dog. He could shake with both paws.

But then he started getting between us in the night, barking us awake. We thought he was being needy. She called him a little shit and rubbed his head. Then something made him snap at her and whine. Both of us were shocked. He was our boy, a good boy.

I took him to a dog psychologist named Bev. She had lots of advice. I sat there and listened and scratched at my arms— around that time my skin starting feeling itchy a lot, but like, from the inside. Eventually she came around to us crating the

74

dog, and I listened, as I'd always been the type to trust the authority of a framed diploma.

We got uninterrupted sleep again. The dog would whine for a bit each night, then calm down, watching us through the bars. As to the itching, which she was feeling too, there was no real concern. We thought maybe bedbugs, but nothing came of it. Life got mostly back to normal.

I woke up first when it happened. They must have agreed my skeleton, being the more daring of the two, would go first. I woke feeling like my arm was asleep, but when I tried to bring the pin-needled gooseflesh of it closer, it wouldn't move. It looked unfull and formless, like a flat tire. My first thought was that I must have been dreaming. Then I felt the first distal phalanx—the tip of my pinky bone—slide up and onto my tongue, followed by the others, followed by my metacarpals, and my mouth was full of slick, gagging panic as the bones of my hand came out, hoisting themselves forward by curling around my jaw.

I made some awful noise, and she woke. The dog whimpered loudly in the corner. She screamed when she saw me, but then was stopped short as her own skeleton started coming out.

Can you imagine? By all means, do. Please, we're begging, take it out of our minds and hold it in your own. Because we don't want it—the agony, the tearing away inside as they got free, the bathrobedness of our bodies, being stepped out of, and all the while the dog going wild. They set him free, by the way, their last small kindness. He licked our faces, nudged at us, and finally left, presumably through the dog door and under the gap in the fence. We don't blame him—he's still our good boy.

You might ask what it means, if it's the manifestation of some metaphor. We ask ourselves too. Not while it was happening, certainly, not as we lost our bone structure, our necessary scaffolding. We were too full of fear, of wondering what would come next. But after, after our skeletons were fully out of us, after they removed the organs from themselves and packed them back down our throats like we were duffel bags, after her skeleton reached over and touched mine where the humerus joins the shoulder, making a dry thocking sound, and after they made their way out of the bedroom and we heard the front door and then the starting car and then heard the last sounds of who we used to be leave us. That's when we started to try and discover what we'd lost and when, precisely, we'd lost it.

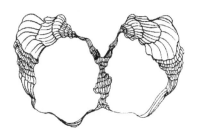

After the accident, she became a kind of confessional. People would come up to her in the hospital bed and whisper into her wound, and in this way they were absolved. The wound would never close, not all the way. There was just too much of it, a jagged hole at her side packed with gauze and weeping. To speak to it is to cleanse one's soul. So the people thought.

The hospital staff tolerated it because a person needs a purpose in life to thrive. She lay there in her near catatonia, occasionally stirring, or wincing, or eating from a tube, as people sought her out. She never reacted to their confessions. She heard them speak, though, felt the words enter her body.

One doctor worried that this was causing her pain because he was in love with her. There was a beauty to her restive face that was oracular. He sat with her most nights, feeling the warmth of her hand in his.

He wasn't a fool. He knew that this was an objectification like any other. Some part of him cared and another part didn't.

Much later, he grew bored and decided she was fine. He didn't know about the pain in her, electric and growing, carving new pathways from wound to limb, arcing through the flesh, the sins of other people making their way along nerve endings and kinking them, snarling up the wires of her body. At the end of it all, he didn't even bother to see it. He thought himself a hero of her story. Isn't it always that way.

INTERROGATION

I will tell you that it started with him eating rocks. The boy, Donald, we could not stop him. And Lord, I tried. His mother tried too. Mostly I believe that. He had read something about birds doing it in a book he'd got for Christmas, and so he started too. I would find him in the yard with a fistful of pebbles, taking them with a glass of water like you might take an aspirin. I slapped them out of his hand, and he bawled toward the sky. That was the first time. I think if I'd acted different he wouldn't have started doing it in secret. I still might have changed the course of events.

I tried so much. I tried reasoning with him. I tried the belt. I tried keeping him indoors. Nothing stopped him. I'd find little piles hidden away. He got handfuls of aquarium gravel, crumbling bits of brick from the side of the house, a whole piece of chalk, which of course is just a rock of a kind. You must understand that there was no talking to the boy once he got something in his head. I put him in that closet for his good. I needed to think, to find a way through to him. It's a failure of imagination, I'll admit. But it kept him safe. I kept him safe.

I think of him in that closet and it's like a womb. Never mind the cobwebbed boxes and the old vacuum cleaner. I thought a room had the meaning you put on it, so I would whisper to him through the bottom that he would be okay, that this was his special safe space. I know he believed it. He didn't have to respond for me to know.

I mean, say you were the interrogant. Say our roles were reversed, and you were sitting in this room, featureless save the ways it has yellowed at the corners, and you were the one being asked about the boy, and you were unfamiliar with the room, so it has a kind of power over you that was told to you by the manner and meaning of the interrogator, the power being a destabilization of self, and say also you knew that this was the purpose of the room—interrogation. Say you knew why you were the one being asked about the boy, that you felt guilty, though of what you did not know, and so you had to wonder if that also was a quality of the room. That perhaps situation and self are one and the same. Say our roles were reversed, and in our reverse roles, you wanted to ask me a question, therefore reversing our reversed roles, and say I allowed you to ask your question. What would it be? Would it be the same as mine? Because my question is this: wouldn't you start to believe you'd done it, whatever it was, since you're here, and here is its own inevitability?

And wouldn't that then be the proof that the boy was saved in there, back in his womb? Wouldn't he be weightless and free?

I can see you are not yet moved, which perhaps proves my point. The boy had never been a talker. He was very nearly a mute. I believe he found language frightening in its livingness, in its ability to shape truth. He liked to read, and he'd ask for dinner, but that was about all. At least around me, at my place. I don't know who he was around his mother. Could've been a different boy entirely, though I don't like dwelling on it. Point is when I put him in that closet he went fully quiet. The boy was just shut off. Which was the idea. I needed to think about this thing with the rocks, and meanwhile I couldn't have him all bellyful of them, sneaking off to some corner to ingest. It scared me. I'll admit that.

When I first told his mother about the rocks, she didn't believe me. That scared me too. Got me to thinking about that different boy that lived with her. And then I thought maybe she was lying, that she'd seen it too. There was never any controlling the woman, which meant there was no controlling the boy in her care. I struggle with it.

I mean, say you were a man who could only be sure of what was in your house? That's every man, isn't it? And what would you do if the thing you loved with everything you had inside you spent more than half the time in a place that you could not be sure of? Meaning: does it even exist in the way you think it does? Meaning: what is not to say that once the boy leaves your sight he is no longer even there? That he might fade out entirely, and a handful of little rocks would plink the ground where he was at the edge of your world, the space you controlled? I have to believe you'd try to stop it in whatever misguided way you could find. I have to believe you'd do it out love, and I have to believe you'd keep the one you loved out of the blooming jaws of that formless unknowing, that same unknowing that led the boy to put a rock on his tongue and think it might transubstantiate into something that would let him fly.

I needed the time to think on the problem, and the more I thought on the problem, the bigger it got in my mind. The boy required a kind of protection I did not know how to give. I thought enough time would allow me a chance at a solution. I needed that time, so I went and made it for myself. I knew his mother would believe me when I said what I said to her, when I told a lie to keep her away and distracted. When she first left me, she said I was a rot on all living things, and that the best thing anyone could do for the future of humanity was to keep away from me. I did not argue because I do not see a point to argument. The judge who awarded joint custody disagreed with her, which was a small mercy in an otherwise ugly time of my life. I will admit her words ring out sometimes in my quietude, like when I'm wandering my property looking for raccoons coming out of the tree line to fuck with my garbage, or when I am hauling a load of scrap metal to sell for weight. My life is not glamourous, and the boy's mother believed that I was cold, unloving, so when I told her the boy ran off she took it for herself and did the rest of the lying for me. I know that likely caused trouble for you all, and for that, I'm sorry. I was only being a good father. I did not do it maliciously, despite the things she has said, the ones I know about, the ones I don't.

I can only assume you have spoken with her, or will be speaking with her soon. Be sure to ask her if you haven't already about her own willingness to believe an untruth so wholly, with a credulousness that seems to me the same as guilt. Because if you are a champion of truth, a susser out of the whole story like I am, an interrogator—which is what you are as I understand it—she stands against you, whereas here I am, compliant.

I kept him in the closet to eliminate the meanwhile. Like, meanwhile, dot dot dot, the boy, dot dot dot, and I wasn't there to keep control on the dot dots. In telling you all this, I am trying to say something profound about love and my behavior. I know you are a skeptic by profession. I know you perhaps think I am confessing to some lesser crime than I've committed, that this is some ploy to turn myself into the victim. I'd ask another question. I'd ask why I'm not a victim, why the world is so eager to move a man out of that category when he's alive like everyone and hurt like everyone and struggling like everyone and going to be one day an object in the ground like everyone.

It was a week he was in there, maybe more. Nine days, maybe. I fed him—granola bars, pancakes, all the flat things he liked I'd slide under the door. I pressed my face to the floor and whispered through the crack that I'd find a way to make it better. He did not answer, not once, but I felt his love and understanding, and a flashlight revealed the outline of his bottom, his feet. My little one safe and sound. I needed him to suspend his belief, just like I need you to suspend yours, to not let the room I'm in be the dictator of the real, just as my boy ultimately did. I want to find him. I believe you do too. I have to.

I know now how perceptive the boy was. He knew that words are not enough to make a room what it is, that it requires something else. Belief, maybe, or just a certain arrangement of matter. Maybe some dance between consciousness and context is required, and it's not just one or the other, and the boy figured that out when I couldn't. Or: maybe he just heard me in my ugliest muttering, and in that way, he knew that he was not in a womb after all. It's a habit I find myself falling back on, talking to myself. I chew my nails to the quick too, till they're beyond bloody. Look at them, all crusted up with the jam of my dried blood. See me. How I feel about all this is written on my body, not guilt but worry. Surely you see it.

Because, see, after that week and a little bit of time, I had my answer. I had turned it over and over in my mind and knew it to be truth. I knew how to make the boy stop eating rocks, how to make him stop believing he might be a bird, how to put him into a state that was both infinite and contained. I knew how to make him fixed is what I'm saying, and though now I don't quite know what I mean, at the time I did, and I girded myself for the act. I went to his womb, and I threw the door open to fix my child, to make things right again.

You know already he wasn't there, so now I have to ask

you how he did it. What kind of will does it take to defy what's real? How do you change context with consciousness? How could a boy misinterpret the world so badly and then end up being correct? Because when I flung the door, he was not there at all. There was no son, no womb, one thing only on the soiled carpet. No boy anymore. Just a pile of rocks.

GUARDIANSHIP

Two angels are fistfighting in my backyard. I watch them through the window, sipping at a gin and grapefruit juice I just made. They, the angels, are naked and smooth and grappling and kidney-punching each other like they really mean harm. Feathers are pulled free. An arm is brutally locked up and bent wrong. They aren't bleeding, but light is pouring out of them in places.

I don't know what they're doing there, or why they're so ferocious—nearly feral—or why they chose my yard, or if I'm supposed to intervene. So: I watch. One of them rears back and headbutts the other, and the other one goes down on the grass. I hear the smack from indoors. The headbutted one gets back up, flapping his wings like a startled chicken.

Dwayne comes out of his room, rumpled but alert. He sees the bottle on the counter.

"You're not supposed to drink that when I'm here," he says, too smart for six, my boy.

"You're supposed to be asleep, so we're both in trouble." I glance from him to the window and back again. One angel grabs the other around the waist and lifts him off his feet, bringing him down hard on the earth.

"Come here," I say, still watching the window. Dwayne walks over to me. I bend down and start messing with his hair. "Look at this. All kinds of wrong. You look like a goddamn dweeb."

He squirms. He winces. He's happy but a part of him isn't, the part of him I never seem to get at in the right way.

"I want to show you something," I say. I hoist him up and show him what's going on in the yard.

"What are they fighting over?" he asks. I can tell he's

afraid, that little boy fear that comes on so easily when he just wakes up, when the world is still here and kept on spinning without his knowledge.

I think on a reason. "They're fighting over us," I say.

"Why?"

"Well, one of them is going to watch over you, and one will watch over me, and they both want to watch over you, so they're fighting to see who gets to look after who."

One of them has the other pinned and is ripping away at his flesh. Dwayne turns away and presses his face into my shoulder. He's never set foot in a church, never read any of the stories. This is his first glimpse of the ugliness inherent in the whole enterprise.

The angel on top stops. The one below him is still, one wing ripped free, the neck turned wrong, light pouring from its mouth and the wounds at its side. The one above has a hand pressed into the face of the one below, and he pulls it away and falls back, shoulders heaving. Soon he will turn and look at us. Soon the next thing will happen, and there's no stopping it. The boy smells of sleep-sweat and fear, his nails dig into me.

"It's love," I say. "It's just love."

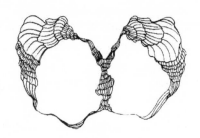

Each morning I find the ghost in a different part of my body. On Monday it hides in the cleft of my collarbone. Tuesday it finds a hair on my shoulder and turns it a shocking white, it unspooled and wiry against the other soft hairs sprouting. I do not pluck it until Wednesday, when the ghost sits in the web between two toes. I need the company. I need to be an object of some melancholy.

My mother is religious. She believes all ghosts are demons, so when she sees the ghost all boogered up in one of my nostrils she tells me to get right or get out. I get out. I borrow three hundred dollars from Tasha, though we've broken up, and she thinks it's a bad idea to keep a ghost like that. She says I might as well get a Bukowski tattoo while I'm at it, that I am hitting peak white boy, that even for me this is and is and et cetera. She hands me the money, though, and says she misses me, sometimes. The ghost makes my ribcage warm.

On the phone, my brother asks, "Whose ghost?" I get into a huff. As though that's the point of a haunting. He asks me what's wrong and I call him a fucking voyeur and then I hang up on him. He's always been so eager to understand something, has always found understanding to be a kind of comfort. Like my mother. Like most.

The ghost. The ghost in the house of my flesh. The ghost next to the bones, reaching in and bespooking the marrow.

The ghost wading in the blood. Nesting in the space between organs. Mewling in my ear. Creaking the doors of me shut in the night. Making me home.

NIGHTHAWK

There's a yellowy light. It's not fluorescent. This is not the IHOP. It's the other one. The local diner. Yellowed sign, yellowed menus, yellow, yellowy light.

—

Nothing that happens here is important. Important is elsewhere is the point of a place like this. This place is meant for in-between.

—

She is at the hostess station looking lost. Looking like a customer who doesn't know if she should seat herself. The post-bar rush is over. A last-call-at-2am town in a last-call-at-2am state. But: it's later than all that. There seems to be no one in the restaurant at all. Bacon grease on everything. Pancakes in the very air.

—

There are some things a body can do, and some things a body cannot do. Some things stand inside the scope, and then some things stand outside the scope, with their mocking smile and wave, with their *cannot*. The sum of these two types of things together is called a person.

—

She has always been an IHOP person, if that's a type of person to be.

—

A man stands up from the one working video poker machine in the corner. This man has a great quality to his hands, prominent knuckles, a meaty rectangular strength to them. There is a tattoo in the webbing between thumb and forefinger—a small cross, hastily done. He wears a maroon polo shirt with a black collar. His hands look capable of doing

88

things to other things, of being *here* and then *here* and then *here* and it helps or it hurts. He waves her along, leading her to a booth by the window. She will not look at his face. She looks at his transitive hands.

—

Notably, the drunks have all gone home for the night.

—

To look at a face is to have a face looked at is to invite comment. She is still beautiful, despite it. She still radiates youth, she still accidentally looks at people in a way that captures their complete attention, despite it. Some things do not change as easily as all that. To say that one thing is the essence of a person is to be naïve. She is in many ways naïve.

—

She sits at a table. She says "Coffee," she says, "Water with no ice." In the blackness of the window she can see herself say these things. The yellow light overhead casts her reflection in dingy ghost shapes. The table lacquer is coming up at one corner, the booth she is sitting in has a slight tear in the seat back. There is damp and ache coming from her breasts. The man leaves her with a menu, which she ignores.

—

A prison doesn't require a key, after all. What it requires is belief in a key.

—

The waiter brings water and disappears again around the corner. Behind her, somewhere, coffee futzes and sputters. He doesn't bother telling her it's brewing. She imagines him on the other side of the wall, playing video poker. On slow nights, a waiter might spend more at the video poker machine than he earns. She thinks he cannot help it. His nametag is peeling, his name rolling back into itself. That it were so easy to disappear, just a furl, a rolling in and away, gone.

—

She finds him, suddenly, boring, wants to stop imagining him. He rubs a dollar against the corner of the video poker, making the money presentable, making it good enough to be accepted by the waiting mouth of the machine. She cannot see it, but this is what he does.

—

Sitting there, she becomes aware of her breathing. She breathes manually, and then she panics that she won't be able to stop breathing manually, that her body will never take over again. How long could she last? How long would it be before that responsibility too became crushing and she let herself collapse gasping to the floor? Could she make it through a cup of coffee, through a meal? Could she make it to daybreak?

—

Never went in for the girl stuff, aside from being deliberate in her beauty. A breath. She thinks of herself as an angular person. A breath. She is all hard edges when she can help it. A breath. Doesn't brook bullshit from anyone. Sees it as strength. A breath. Was not this for a time. A breath. And now. A breath.

—

There's an old joke, and it's this: What's the worst thing that can happen in a falling elevator? It stops. And what's the best thing? It stops. Which isn't funny, so maybe it's not a joke. But it's true.

—

She tries to calm herself the way she was taught by her college roommate years ago: breathe out twice as long as you breathe in, count it out, name three things you love about being alive, realize that you are only your body, or realize that you are not just your body—she couldn't remember which it was or if it was both—just ride the wave, live through this and then this and then this and guess what: now you're living, present tense and actual. Now you're now.

—

It could be said fairly that every moment is life-changing, each insuck of air irrevocable. Thoughts like these are banal at every moment they aren't.

—

Three things she loves about being alive:

—

The waiter reappears, passes her, returns with coffee. The presence of him forces her to be calm. She sits. She sips her coffee. It is surprisingly good. She expected something over-roasted, bile-sour, stale. Something that cried out for the little tub of cream in its basket on the table, sitting by the plastic tower of assorted jellies. There is a kind of betrayal in the robust flavor, in how good it feels to put the warmth into her body.

—

From the video poker machine, bleeps and bloops move softly through the dining area.

—

There is an absence of need in her that's new, or worse, long-forgotten, the mark of an earlier version of herself pupating within her, ready to reemerge. She opens a tub of cream and dumps it in, then another. The coffee grays and whorls. It blooms. The way the black outside snugs up on the windows makes her feel as though she is attenuated to bigger truths lurking in the mundane. She wants things to be this still for her from now on.

—

She might be connected to something new. A great heritage of loneliness. Nighthawk. That one Hemingway story she hated so much. Aaron made her read it in college, Aaron who got so upset when she didn't care about all the *nada*, when she found it too cliché to be interesting. At the time she felt so sorry to hate the story. How often had she been sorry for her own opinion?

—

She is not quite sure what it will be like, what she will do with so many empty hours, if it will ever feel as though this is what life is instead of feeling like, well, like what, exactly? Like she's her own ghost, staying behind, carrying on.

—

A body is still a vessel when it holds only itself. She learned this when the baby was born, and then somewhere she unlearned it, as the baby began to grow and occupy more space, kept finding more space to occupy than she knew was even there in her to occupy. It's a thing she'd like to know again: how much space can fit in the vessel.

—

She trembled and slipped back into breathless panic. She thought *I fucking told you.* She thought *Do not think about the Pollywog.* She thought *She didn't cry when you set her car seat down on pavement, when you hurried away.* She thought *She stayed right asleep that scary way the Pollywog would sleep, scary baby too-deep sleep.*

—

The waiter comes back around to see if she's ready. She apologizes. She forgot about the menu in front of her. He looks over his shoulder to the kitchen and says it's fine. She is overly apologetic. He says it's okay, but she persists in performing the act of apology, fingers squirming at the menu.

92

—

In some ways she will always be in that two-bedroom apartment, man and baby and her as ghost. She does not want to know this, but she does.

—

The waiter lingers. The waiter notices the quaver of her and wants to help. He asks her where she's from and she says, "Here." He puts two fingers on the table. He says, "No, I mean your peoples." And she is looking at him, fierce, reddened eyes. He's from somewhere too, by the look of him. "Guatemala," she says, "Libya." He whistles and says, "That's some mix." Her shoulders tighten. She does not want to talk to a waiter about anything, least of all this. That a person can reach adulthood without knowing this kind of small talk is terrible, sticking your finger in another person's nose.

—

She does not want to be hard angles right now, but she is with the waiter. She wants to be a *not*. She thinks she might unwrap her fork from its napkin and jab his fingers off the table. He stands there, not letting her be a *not*, forcing her to be a person in a context that came from somewhere. It's horrible. He's horrible.

—

An in-between is a place like any other. Everybody lives in the present, all the time. Horrible.

—

She was not always this woman. She learned to be another woman with Aaron. Aaron saw different because Aaron wanted her to love him, wanted that plain, and that came with a desire to bend the will of her to his, get her, the organism, a little closer to *her*, the idea in his mind. She's not that idea, though. Not that she blames him. She did it, too, though not so much with Aaron. Aaron was Aaron, without consequence. She did it with the Pollywog. She did it until she realized she couldn't.

—

With Aaron she saw she could be not unhappy. Which is nothing at all like happy.

—

Three things she loves about being alive:

—

She takes a deep drag on the cigarette and her lungs fuzz out. Somewhere a baby wakes in the cold. Somewhere a baby. Somewhere a loss without language. Somewhere a light going on at the precinct, a savior arriving, not the wanted one. Somewhere a vessel being made unwhole.

—

But who has ever been whole. It's there in the word itself. Whole, hole. Cruelty, homonym.

—

Three things she loves about being alive:

—

That coffee goes cold. That dawn comes on. That a different now is on the way.

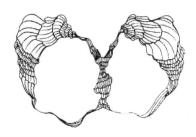

He plucked out a rib and fed it to his daughter, and in this way, she grew strong enough and left him. He watched her gnaw meat from bone, tearing, lips of his lips, teeth of his teeth, and then she turned away and was gone. This is the way of children, but he was not expecting it, and the surprise was not something he knew how to articulate. Instead, he hurt her whenever he could, however he was able. She had eaten of his body, after all, and owed.

Mostly this took the form of the common cruelties that exist there at the intersection of fathers and capitalism— disappointment, picking at the wounds of girlhood, spending the time she visited home locked in his garage. This story is not a story about the mostly. This is a story of particular cruelty.

When she wasn't paying attention, he snuck up on her, turned her around, and made her live in reverse. This was in the morning, just before a holiday breakfast. She went back to sleep, woke up at night. She lived the previous day, dusk to dawn. And the previous. And so on. It was awful, the unwomaning of her. The girling.

She hated him for it but couldn't stop it, couldn't find a way to break loose of time/fathers. Escaping from time/fathers takes a lifetime, which is what he had stolen from her.

They arrived together at the moment when he plucked a part of himself and offered it up. He believed he had some small decency, and so he had lived in reverse too, mourning what he had taken even as he took it, accepting the rib and placing it back inside of himself, letting her continue then backward, letting her be unmade, the world not allowed its portion of damage and grace. The world had its cruelty and he had his own and his was stronger, believing himself somehow outside of that world, the world not allowed to have her, and her the world. This is a father.

THE PRE-INTERVIEW PHASE

Thank you for your application to job posting #11394 – Fondness Technician. Congratulations on making it to phase two of the application process! The following supplemental questions are designed to both orient you with the needs of the position and to give us, the company, a better feel for who you, the applicant, are and hope to be. Your answers are important to us. Please consider each question and respond with care.

    1.   Define as many kinds of affection as you are able.

    2.   Did you forget any, or are some of them on the tip of tongue and you are embarrassed that you can't remember? Or are some of them too personal for you to write down? (Don't be shy—you're doing fine. Shyness is, after all, one sign of a low-level fondness of the potential revealer for the potential revealee).

    3.   Do you have any dead pets or grandparents from your childhood or adolescent years that you recall fondly? Please list them below.

    4.   Do your grandparents—living or dead—hold any outdated and perhaps uncomfortable notions about race, gender and/or sexuality, mandatory coupling, infant-control hormone therapy, or the focused application of positive energy in the corporate workplace?

    4a. Do you love them just the same? (If some other factor frustrated or otherwise tempered your love for them, please describe it below)

    5.   Have you ever felt fondness for an inanimate

object?

5a. If the answer to 5 is yes, please rate your fondness on a scale of 1-10. If no, continue to question 6.

5b. If the answer to 5a is above a 6, please answer the following: have you ever felt such fondness for an inanimate object that you have used it in an act of self-pleasure (excluding objects that are explicitly designed for that purpose)? If no, continue to question 6.

5c. If the answer to 5b is yes, please thoroughly describe the object. If no, continue to question 6.

6. What was your fondest childhood toy or object? (If the answer is the same as question 5c, write "please see 5c").

7. How did you use your fondest childhood toy or object? Was it primarily enjoyed visually, tactilely, etc.? Did it require the use of transitive verbs to enjoy?

8. Do you have children? If yes, please skip question 9.

9. Do you ever miss children that do not exist?

9a. If the answer to question 9 is yes, do you ever feel guilty about this?

9b. If the answer to question 9a is yes, is the guilt rooted in your own childlessness (which would be, after all, a sign of your failure to participate in the great human project), or in the fondness you feel for a non-entity, or in your enjoyment of your childlessness, or is there some other reason?

10. If you see a domestic animal in the street, do you pick it up, look for its owner, avoid contact, or other?

11. Describe the crime you witnessed on the way to the exam site this morning.

11a. Who did you side with?

11b. Why did the mugger mug that young woman?

11c. In your opinion, did the mugger choose the right victim?

12. Do you own or know where to find a weapon?

12a. If the answer to 12 is yes, please describe how you feel imagining the weapon in your hand. If the answer is no, please move to question 13.

13. Have you ever felt depressed?

14. Have you felt any of the following symptoms in the past six months? (check all that apply)

a. Trouble sleeping

b. Night terrors

c. A feeling that the inherent meaninglessness of existence makes continued striving pointless in and of itself

d. Acid reflux, post-nasal drip, migraines, or any other recurring malady that occurs more frequently than you feel is normal or justified (please explain in the space provided)

e. Overeating

f. Undereating

g. A desire to hold a baby bird in your hands and squeeze until it feels like a soft bag of broken matchsticks in your palm

      h.   A feeling that you might ultimately be vestigial

      i.   Frequent gas or bloating

15. If given access to a computer terminal displaying a photograph of a human being, how confident are you that you could fall in love with said human being (please answer on a scale of 1-10).

      15a. Do you think answering that question in the hypothetical is entirely meaningless, mostly meaningless, or other?

      15b. Explain how you would know that you are in love with the actual person, and not the idea of the person, the photograph itself, or the computer terminal.

16. Do you think that self-gratification while thinking fondly of someone is a demonstration or furtherance of that fondness?

17. How do you feel about us, the company?

18. Is that different than you feel about the individual or individuals who wrote these questions? Please explain your answer.

19. Define cognitive dissonance.

20. Define cognitive assonance.

21. How far are you willing to go to make questions 19 and 20 have the same answer?

22. Outline a plan to go even farther than that.

THE NEW OLD WEST

The ghosts were browsing tonight, picking through the off-color knickknacks and refrigerator magnets. Truth told it was more annoying than spooky. Trent, my manager, worried after them constantly. He swatted at them with a cheapie electric bug swatter that he'd paid for and unwrapped for the very purpose. It looked like a tennis racket and was emblazoned with the words *Skeeter Defeater*.

It was an ungodly hot summer night and I'd rolled my short sleeves up on my shoulders and he came over and tapped me on a shoulder with the damn thing and it stung.

"God, fuck, Trent."

"Gotta stay in uniform, Jen."

"I am in uniform."

His nose hair bristled. "Sleeves down. Be professional."

I looked around. Aside from the ghosts, of which there were three or four, there was no one else here. One of the ghosts was trying repeatedly to pick up a ceramic eagle statue. From the frustrated look of him, when living he was the kind of person who wanted to speak to the manager.

Trent ran over there and whipped the Skeeter Defeater around. It passed right through the ghost, swirling him up a little bit. The ghost threw his hands up in exasperation and walked off. Sweat slid down my back. I looked at the ghost by the coffee mugs and gave her a look of *well whatever*. Aside from occasionally submitting to being shooed off, the ghosts never interacted with us. Still, she was one of the ones I liked. She had a classic ghost look—long, braided hair, flowy dress, barefoot. I thought if we could just have conversation together, it would be lovely. My life in Abilene would finally pass the Bechdel test. I sipped at my sweet tea.

With Trent out here, I couldn't read and I couldn't sneak outside to smoke and I couldn't change the music and then lip sync into a magic marker for the ghosts. The only thing I could do was wallow and listen to the air conditioner struggle and fail.

The New Old West Rest Stop and Restaurant was in a sorry state these days. The restaurant and mini golf course were both closed down. No one was allowed to take the stairs up to the top of the giant cowboy hat anymore. Now it sat there atop its fake oil derrick, its paint going pale from the sun, being mistaken for a riff on the Eiffel Tower. Tourists would stop and ask if this was Paris, TX. When I told them it was just Abilene, their faces would sink. I went up there once and it was like you could see nearly to Oklahoma.

The only things that were still open were the snack bar, the gas station, and the gift shop, and I bounced between all three as needed. The fireworks stand had been open for the 4th, which was marked by Trent buying a box of snappers and flicking them at my feet when I wasn't paying attention. Trent's management style left something to be desired.

During the day people came in, and the shop did decent business selling tacky cowboy and Americana memorabilia *hecho en Mexico*—refrigerator magnets of snoozing caballeros under massive sombreros, tin coyotes howling at the moon, that kind of stuff. I couldn't imagine owning any of it, but people came in to use the bathroom and ended walking out with at least a *Don't Mess with Texas* coffee mug. It sort of blew my mind. Growing up, I'd hated Abilene and the surrounding plains and, by extension, anyone with even a shred of outsized Texas pride. And yeah, maybe I secretly enjoyed seeing the cowboy hat lit up and buzzing from my window in the back bedroom of the trailer, and maybe when

I was staying up with the window open blowing out weed vapor through the screen (old habits from when I smoked joints and had to be extra careful of my moms and my brother Denny finding out), a highlighter between the pages of a Judith Butler book, I'd see some nice stars I imagine you didn't get a good look at from New York or Chicago. Still didn't change the dead grass and the duststorm grime on everything, the prehistoric derricks pumping, the cow shit.

Once the sun went down, traffic to the gift shop sort of slowed to a trickle, since the New Old West sold gas for ten cents above what every station in Abilene did. We stayed open until midnight for some reason, with nothing but the ghosts and the occasional teenager coming in to swipe a bottle opener or buy cigarettes.

Trent went out back to smoke. I walked over to one of the ghosts, a doughy man in a grease-stained shirt. The air around him smelled faintly of earwax, funk. He didn't look up from the CD rack. He was staring at the back of a Bonnie Raitt's *Nick of Time*. I could tell by looking at him that he'd been one of the ones in the gas-well explosion. One of our newer ghosts. There were several. No matter how good my eyesight, I couldn't ever make out which ghost it was until I got up close. Something about their spectral nature. If I went outside and stood in the parking lot looking in, I wouldn't be able to see him at all.

"I'm Jen," I said. The ghost seemed to flinch but didn't look up.

"I bet it's pretty lonely. You guys never talk to each other."

The ghost tried to turn the rack, and his hand passed through it. I reached over and twirled it a quarter of the way around for him. He looked confused, a little lost.

"Probably I'm just projecting."

. . .

When my shift was over, I saw a bunch of ghosts posing in front of the fiberglass cowboy out front. The cowboy is twice their height—his bow legs making a rainbow that joins at his crotch, one arm thrust through a beltloop, the other firing a gun wildly in the air. His chipped paint makes him look leprous, but still a couple people take a photo with him each day. Sometimes they paw at his groin or mime blowing him.

"Hey, could you take our picture?" one of them asked, and it startled me. I looked up from my phone. One of the ghosts was alive, a girl in a purple tank top and board shorts.

"Sure," I said, and held out my hand for her phone. The ghosts smiled passively. One of them held up bunny ears for no one.

"Oh," the girl said. "I don't have a real phone." She pointed toward the ghosts arranged behind her. "I just thought, you know, it seems like it matters to them."

"Oh, okay." I held up my phone to take the picture.

"I'm trying to have empathy for others," the girl said. "Like as a philosophy."

She stepped back among the ghosts and smiled. One of her eyeteeth had grown in above where it should have and jutted out at a bit of an angle. I took the photo.

She hopped forward. "Did they turn up?"

I shook my head without even looking at my phone to see. "They never do."

She looked back at them. "Hmm. I guess if that's their unfinished business, it's got to stay unfinished."

She smiled at her own joke, and I put my phone away and looked back toward the store. Trent clicked the lights off, leaving the two of us lit only by the orangey buzzing neon above us.

"Did you want me to send you the picture?" I asked.

"Nah," she said, looking back at the ghosts. "If it's just me, I don't see much point."

We stood there for a moment, neither of us sure what to do. Then Trent came out the front door and started locking it. She stepped away with a half-hearted wave and walked off to a car at the end of the parking lot.

At home, Denny was still awake, watching a superhero movie on the TV that took up the whole back wall of the trailer. My moms was asleep in her robe on the couch, an empty six-pack arranged around her like votive candles to some ageless saint.

"Go to bed, Denny."

He barely turned to me. "I am in bed." Which was true— his foam pad and his sleeping bag were arranged around him. When I moved back home, mom had moved from the back bedroom to the couch, leaving Denny without a real place to sleep. They'd downgraded to the trailer to help me with tuition, and now we were all stuck here through the year at least, more if we didn't find a way to pay my hospital bills. Denny's sleeping bag, like most of the stuff around here, was the kind of temporary situation that everyone knew was permanent. It was mom's misguided but kind opinion that a person on suicide watch needed a space to herself.

I put my hand on his head. "You have school tomorrow?"

"I have to go, but it's a test day for the stupid kids."

"Don't be mean." Denny was in the gifted program, and he'd started to become a little bit of a shit since he'd noticed the mustache hairs coming in at the corners of his mouth. Next year was junior high for him

"They can't hear me."

"Still." I scrunched up his scalp with my fingers, feeling a little bad for him. He'd get through his whole childhood never having to do anything hard, and then somewhere in early adulthood something was gonna come along and kick his teeth right in. Whether it was school or a job or a lover didn't much matter. He spent his days dissecting owl pellets, writing poetry. He was all-the-way doomed.

He pointed to the TV screen. "You seen this one?"

"I'm American, aren't I?"

On the screen, a woman was tied to a chair, covered in grime. The villain threatened her with a long knife, and the leering grin on his face doubled down on the implicit metaphor. Soon she would be rescued, she would kiss the hero, and et cetera. She may as well have been a piece of stationary with doodled tits and the word *plot* written across it.

"Why do you watch this crap?"

Denny looked up at me, grinning. "I'm American, aren't I?"

"Cute."

I left him there and went to the back bedroom. The salt lamp was on, giving the room a soft glow. I moved some textbooks off of the bed. I'd taken incompletes at Texas Woman's University—my professors were all kind about it and said to contact them in the fall to finish up the coursework. I think they knew I wasn't coming back. I mean, it's not like it was a hard situation to read—gone two weeks, then showing up in front of them with a bandaged wrist and a form to sign without making eye contact. One of them hugged me and patted my back. I kept poking through the books. It was something to do.

I fished my phone out of my pocket and looked at the picture. The flash on my phone had washed out the girl's features, and she looked a little startled and pathetic standing there by herself. I thought of deleting it, but didn't. I looked through some pictures from the fall semester. I'd been happy when I took them, but now they all seemed pretty uninteresting and a little sad. I flipped back to the girl and her ghosts and decided she didn't look pathetic after all. She looked happy.

I scrubbed my face and tossed the wipe in the trash bin. Mom's bed—my bed—was lumpy, and it gathered all around me. It was too hot in the trailer. The TV's muffled and empty talk. The salt lamp's glow. Sleep coming on uneasy. A roomful of my mother's things stuffed into a corner. Down the road a ways the cowboy hat jutting into the sky atop its oil derrick tower. All of it mostly useless, and me too.

Two nights later, the girl was back. She came inside this time, wearing a backpack that was covered in buttons and patches and a flowy, flowery skirt. Trent was nowhere to be seen.

"Hey," I called out. It came out kinda mean sounding, and she looked startled. A ghost was sitting on the floor between us, cleaning ghost dirt from his fingernails.

"Hey," she said, stepping carefully over the ghost and making her way to the counter.

"You can just walk through them," I said. "They don't mind it."

She looked back behind her at the ghost. "How do you

107

know?"

The question was embarrassing, and I crossed my arms in front of me. I knew because I knew, because I'd gotten most of the way there. The scar on my left wrist wasn't even that noticeable, but I did what I could to hide it. "I guess I don't."

She set the bag on the counter between us and opened it. Inside was a thermos and a sandwich.

"I don't know if you like coffee, or if it's too hot for it. But here. And the sandwich is peanut butter and jelly, because you look like you might be a vegan."

She set them on the counter. I didn't know what to do, so I sort of frowned at the air in front of us.

She stepped back. "Oh god. Do you have a nut allergy?"

"What? No. I just, what the hell is this?"

"It's dinner? For you?"

I eyed the sandwich and the coffee. "I'm not a lesbian, if that's what you're thinking."

She shrugged. "Part of empathy is it makes no assumptions."

I picked up the coffee and took a sip. It was too hot, and I was already sweating anyway. "I'm not a charity case either."

"Didn't say you were." She leaned forward onto the counter. "I'm Spence. Spencer."

"Jen."

Her name struck me odd. As close as we were, I could see the way her hair came down into sideburns a little in front of her ears, the padded bra. *Oh,* I thought. Her being transgender was a surprise, if only because it didn't seem like something that would occur to someone living in Abilene, the reddest part of a very red state. Suddenly everything I was thinking and doing seemed wrong. I had clocked them, had pronouned and gendered them, had assumed. And then there was that their correcting my wrongness was emotional labor they may not want to do, that wasn't their burden, and my knowing that and not being sure what to do about it somehow made me both more and less complicit in the crimes of the patriarchy. And even switching to gender neutral pronouns in my mind seemed like a violence of a sort, marking the difference between us.

None of this was Spencer's problem.

She could tell that I was uncomfortable, so she said, "Is it okay if I try again with the ghosts?"

"Yeah, go nuts."

"Cool. I hope you like the sandwich."

She walked away from the counter, toward the wall of refrigerator magnets stuck to a piece of sheet metal. One of the ghosts was scanning them up and down, and Spence put her hand on his shoulder, holding it there as though the ghost might bear her weight. She picked a magnet off the wall and held it out to the ghost, turning it over and letting him see the price tag. The ghost ignored her, but I was fascinated in watching Spence's body in a way that reminded me that I wasn't as progressive and cool as I thought. I mean, I'd gone to a woman's college in a liberal town. Was I this hung up on a person's genitals as a determining factor?

Probably yes.

I had time to reflect on this as she went from ghost to ghost, trying to help them some way. Nobody came to see the ghosts at the New Old West. They'd begun to show up in the 80s, after the interstate bypass made us into a detour instead of a mandatory stop. The ghosts were all the recent dead, and the unspoken consensus among the ghost hunting community after a few tepid visits was that it wasn't worth the drive out without the sense of mystery and romance.

Nobody likes a ghost in coveralls and a Skynyrd shirt.

Well, nobody but Spence, apparently, who was currently wrapping one up in a hug. It seemed a frustrating thing to do, but I guess she's used to frustration, used to things being not as they should be but as they are.

Shut the fuck up, Jen. She's a regular person.

I pulled the sandwich from its baggie. The bread was smushed, and there was too much peanut butter on it, so it gummed up in my mouth. Trent was napping in the backroom. Since I'd been back in town, I'd been waiting for something inside of me to change drastically, but so far all that had happened was I'd given up shaving my legs. I thought that being alive meant that sometimes there was a hard shift inside of you. I'd heard of people changing their minds about things, having sudden revelations, and they always described it as something profound. To me it had always seemed like I was just spackling over what had come before, that everything inside me was just getting cruddier and cruddier. Well, and here I was waiting for that clean break with peanut butter sticking hard in my throat and sweat darkening my shirt, and I'd keep waiting, probably.

Spence looked over and gave me a thumbs up. Her cheerfulness was forced. It was easy enough to see that. Still, it seemed like she meant it.

Right before midnight, Spence bought a twelve of Corona and a pack of menthols. When we closed, she was sitting against the side of the building in the little strip of good pavement. The rest of the parking lot was loose gravel. She clinked the cement beside her with her beer and invited me to sit. I did, and she handed me a beer of my own, set the cigarettes between us.

We sat like that awhile. I smoked two cigarettes back to back. Her calves were toned, smooth. There was a tattoo on one of them that it was too dark to make out. Trent came out and scowled at us and then left. I was not a chit-chatter. I was never good at it, and I'd been friendless for some time, so I was even more out of practice. I said the only thing I could think to say:

"When did you know you were a woman?"

Spence looked at me like *Oh, how precious* and said, "When did you decide you wanted to stay alive?"

I lit a cigarette and dug a heel into the gravel.

"I meant really," she said. "I know it's kind of a lurid question, but I think people shouldn't be so afraid of themselves." She held out her hand for the lighter, and I gave it over. "I'll trade you. Secret for secret."

I sighed out a lungful of smoke and prepped for the lie. "Pretty much immediately after I did the thing. I think about it now and I think it wasn't so much I wanted to die as that I wanted an excuse to leave school."

"Why?" She'd crossed her legs and turned toward me.

"It all seemed so pointless. I mean, I know that sounds like a depressed person's reason, and it is, and I know that, and whatever, but think about it. The nation and the environment are in freefall, cruelty keeps getting bigger and louder, there's no real purpose or pleasure in goal-making, and here I am taking women's studies classes when really what everyone seems to be saying with their talk of empowerment and equality was 'This is a losing battle, and you might get raped along the way, so squeeze the legs tight.' And that's why I bought the knife in the first place, because I felt I would have cause to use it on someone else, and I guess it kind of seemed like a romantic notion to turn it on myself so I could go home again, maybe get to a place where I could unknow some of this shit."

I didn't say the rest. I didn't say how it had been like I said when I had planned it all out, a decision that seemed based in intellect and wholly rational. Like it was an escape hatch, a way to reset everything. But then, I sat there after the cut, which had been near impossible to do—the body has an almost magnetic impulse against self-harm—and decided that it wasn't a cry for help after all. That I'd been kidding myself about going home, that what I'd really wanted was an end, and so I closed my eyes and threw my phone across the bathroom, smashing it. It was spring break, and the dorms were abandoned, and without the phone I was committed to the act. And when I slipped under, there was no light, there was no clarity of thought or being. There was a warmth nearby in the dark, the heat coming from beyond a threshold, and then there were hands against me, pushing me away, keeping me from the door. I'd wanted to go through. I'd cried out, begging them to let me in the door, to give me something like relief, even if it was just a long silence. If I couldn't have a happy ending—and who could—I at least wanted one that was my own. Sometimes I still do.

Spence put her hand on my knee and said, "I was like eight or nine when I knew I was a girl. There wasn't much to it. My parents are weirdly supportive. It's like a nonissue in my house."

"I guess I win."

A ghost tripped over a rock and fell face first in the gravel.

"Now why do you think they can touch the ground like that but can't pick up a postcard?" Spence asked.

"You are asking the wrong person."

"It's just bizarre is all."

I watched him push himself up to a sitting position and dust off his hands. He seemed resigned to who he was.

"I don't think you can solve their problems, you know," I said. "I think their existence is pretty much problem-free. I think maybe this is just where they want to be." Of course I was talking about myself. That's what happens all the time with conversations about ghosts.

"That seems even sadder." Spence had her eyes closed, and she wasn't paying much attention anymore. There were more empty beers around us than I expected.

"I don't know," I said, trying to keep the hurt out of my voice.

Spence leaned over into me and kissed my shoulder before putting her head on it. I flinched and she didn't notice.

Denny was on the stoop making confetti from the nearly dead basil plant when we got there. I couldn't think of the last time any one of us had cooked a meal more involved than box macaroni, but mom kept buying and then neglecting live herbs anyway.

"Hey, squirt."

"Hey."

"Mom around?"

"She's in town with Greg."

It was well past one. I frowned, though this wasn't really new.

"She feed you before she went?"

"I got pizza."

Denny and I were practiced in the art of ignoring each other's friends, so I made no attempt to introduce Spence.

Instead, we walked past him and into the trailer. The pizza was sitting on the coffee table, and I grabbed a slice and gestured to Spence that she could have some if she wanted. While I ate, I kicked Denny's dirty laundry into the corner and pushed the blankets aside to make room on the couch. I swapped what was left of the Coronas for a fresh case of beer from the fridge and set it on the table in front of us.

We sat around drinking beers and fidgeting in half-comfortable silence for an hour. I turned on the TV and we watched a rerun of *Cheaters*. It was all clearly staged. Spence put her hand on my knee. I let her. At some point, Denny came in and got a soda and went back outside. He should've been asleep, but it was almost summer break for him, and it was the weekend, and Denny wasn't the kind of kid to cause real trouble. Plus: not his mother.

Spence shifted toward me and her hand moved up my leg some. I didn't think I really wanted to kiss her, but I did anyway, like how sometimes it's just the next thing and the next and the next. She had one hand on my leg and the other behind my neck and then that one went down my arm and her thumb brushed the scar and we stopped.

"Sorry," she said.

I wanted to say *For what*, but I didn't. I knew I was maybe kind of a project, for her and for everybody. I put my hand on her other hand and moved it all the way up so that it was pressing against me through my jeans and we did that awhile. What I wanted was to be into it. What I wanted was a cleansing kind of focus, I wanted to feel like a semi truck juddering down a mountain in the dark, but that's not what it was. I mean, I liked the attention, but it didn't get me anywhere is all.

Sometimes I felt like an open wound in the world's skin.

I know that's cheap as metaphor goes.

I pulled her hand away. She looked at me all puppy-cute and timid. I felt heavy-headed from the beer. I wasn't supposed to drink with my antidepressant.

"What?" she said.

"Nothing."

The next night at work while Spence was wandering around being nice to the ghosts, Trent walked up to me looking more irritated than usual.

"Does he buy things ever?"

"Sometimes."

He gnawed on the end of his ratty moustache. "You're a bad liar, Jen."

I looked at my fingernails and waited. One of the ways to deal with Trent was to let him run his own course.

"Listen," he said, "I don't like it, but Brandon Mosskey's got enough trouble without me kicking his faggy son out of my shop."

Spence was talking to a ghost in soothing tones. I knew well enough that Trent was beyond correction. Or else I was a coward who didn't stick up for her friends. Or else there was still some part of me that still saw Spence the same way as Trent did—just some faggy boy who needed ironing out. Heat went into my face. I knew I had to say something.

"Spence is his daughter."

Trent snorted. "Whatever you want. Brandon says he ain't got no kid at all, so at this point it's all theoretic."

Trent was beyond guile, and he was more ignorant than mean-spirited, so I knew he was telling the truth. Spence was not welcome in her family. Probably she wasn't welcome much anywhere, especially not in this town. Hence here, among the ghosts.

My face was getting hotter, and I said, "Don't fire me Trent, but fuck you."

Trent put his hands up. "Look, I'm just telling you how it is. He can stick around all he likes, but tell him he's got to buy something now and again. I've got enough loiterers that I can't do anything about."

I kept my mouth shut and glared at him. *What does she matter to you?* popped into my head. I didn't know who the question was for.

That night Spence and I sat in the wide mouth of the plaster hippo that marked the last hole of the mini golf course. We dropped our empty beers and our cigarette butts down the back of its throat into the ball compartment beneath that was rusted shut. The turf around us was patchy and gone in most places. The ghosts wandered the course, too—they had the run of the whole place but never seemed to go that far past the mini golf. A few hung out at the abandoned motel and restaurant beyond the neon's glow, but most of them seemed to stay near the gift shop. Of course, so did I.

One of them was squatting down at the head of the eighteenth hole, gauging the shot, meaning it looked like he was staring right at us. I shooed at him with my free hand, and Spence stopped me.

"Leave him be," and then, to the ghost, "Go ahead and play through, buddy. We won't stop you."

He ignored us. I thought of the word *buddy* as a mannish thing to say, like *dude* or *broseph*. Then I thought, *well, do you micro-manage your own behavior all the time, Jen?* I sat and watched the ghost with Spence and got more thoroughly drunk.

When the ghost moved on, we kissed a little and then stopped.

"What are you thinking?" she asked.

"I guess I wasn't." We sat in silence for a minute or more. "What were you thinking?"

"Just, like, the ghosts. How they don't react to us at all. And how that's maybe more honest."

"More honest than what?"

"Than what everyone else does. Like, how we act like we understand each other when we talk, and like we actually see and feel for one another, when what we're looking at is our own reflected whatever it is coming right back at us."

My head felt full up with sand. "I've read something like this. At school."

After a minute I said, "You're saying empathy is just a kind of self-pity."

"I don't know what I'm saying." She sighed and looked away. "I just like you, Jen, is all."

She put her hand on my leg. Both of us waited to see what would happen next. Finally I said, "I'm pretty fucked up as people go. Maybe you should just kiss me some more."

She did, and we did that a while. She kissed like she was trying to figure me out, what I liked, what I didn't. Her hands went places, never staying anywhere for long. I enjoyed her attention. I let her do her thing. Still, something kept me walled off. Maybe she was right about empathy and connection. Some of the stuff she was doing I enjoyed, but I didn't react. I let her keep searching. I pretended I was one of the ghosts, and she was trying to reach me somehow. A part of me thought *You wouldn't have been here for this if they'd let you through the door. You feel numb now, but you don't even know.*

I stopped her and stood up. "Come on." I offered her my hand. We went around to the back of the gift shop, where there was a little storage shed. Inside there was a shovel, a toolbox, a push mower. I grabbed the shovel.

"What are we doing?" she asked.

"Climbing the hat."

We went back outside. The oil derrick and the cowboy hat loomed over us. It stood a little apart from the gift shop, fenced in by chain link topped with razor wire.

I said, "It used to be they let anybody go up here, but then the stairs started rusting out. You ever been up?"

Spence nodded. "I think I was eight or nine."

"Well, you've never been at night."

The gate was secured by light-gauge chain and a fairly cheap looking Masterlock knock-off. I put the blade of the shovel between the fence gate and the fence proper and leaned into it with my whole body. It took two or three tries before the chain popped and started loose.

"Jesus, Jen," Spence said. "You're gonna get fired."

"We've got plenty of hooligans around here to blame it on. I'll be fine." Part of me knew that Trent would blame Spence, that she'd be banned from the store, or Trent would go to her dad, and who knows what else from there. Spence would forgive me for it if it went down that way, probably. I didn't care. It felt good being selfish, doing exactly what I wanted. I leaned in again with the shovel, levering the gate open enough for me to slip inside.

The door to the stairs had a proper latch, but I knew it wasn't locked. I held it open for Spence. Spence came through the gate and kissed me on the way through the door.

"I'm not kidding about the stairs," I said. "Hold the rail tight."

We started up. The stairs wound around the inside of the tower for fifty feet or so before reaching a little hatch to a viewing deck that was railed off from the cowboy hat's brim. For the first few flights they were lit by the lights of the parking lot, but once we got above them it was impossible to see clearly where we were stepping. We went slowly. I felt thoroughly drunk. Even at this late hour, it was in the nineties, but there was a breeze that felt pleasant, the hot breath of scrub country.

I watched Spence as she climbed. There was a world of mystery in the shadows of her body, in the body itself. It had nothing to do with her being transgender—it was about being a person, weird and broken and unknown, and her identity just sort of underlined all that some. I thought about things the doctor said I was supposed to let go of: feeling like I was meaningless, and that that was a part of both who I was and the inescapable truth of every person. My mom abandoning Denny to his own devices, and how I was ready to do that too. Denny growing up warped and rootless, the wood of him dry and split in the sun. That I belong here in Abilene, somehow, that I belong in a place that seems so empty. By the time we reached the top, I'd been through most all of what the doctor called *hands-off topics* and found that, at least right now, they weren't as scary as I thought.

The hatch was a little rusty but gave with a shove. We hoisted ourselves over and were on the viewing deck, which was a corrugated steel floor that ran around the whole north side of the hat. It was walled off by the fiberglass brim of the hat on one side and a railing that prevented people from stepping onto the hat proper on each end. We leaned against the brim and looked back out toward Abilene. Spence whistled, impressed. We smoked a cigarette between us.

"It's almost a nice place, seeing it like this," I said.

"Almost."

There wasn't much of a moon, so that if you weren't looking toward the lights of Abilene, it was as if the tower were an outpost at the end of existence. Just a half-formed black beyond it, the West. I thought of the people who used to just get in their car and go, off to Roswell, or Santa Fe, or Vegas, or the Grand Canyon, or California, how even after it became a cliché, o pioneers and all that, it got so close to a real kind of meaning, looking for the boundary of who you were and who you might be if only you could hold on, if only there was enough road to cover the gap between the two.

I thought of Judith Butler and de Beauvoir and bell hooks and Maggie Nelson and my mother and of Spence. Someone somewhere would find an answer for all of this. The work toward some profound solution was happening right in that moment. Meanwhile, I walked to the edge of the railing and took a step up on it, straddled it, and was over. The fiberglass of the cowboy hat flexed beneath me like it might give out. Spence shouted at me to come back. I told her it was okay, that everything was fine, that nothing bad could happen. I walked out to the edge. Everything is a fight, a push and a pushback of all possible truths. There's no clean break of a changed mind coming for me because a person isn't hard like that. A person is just muck and thought. That's being alive. It was like an addiction that way, where you can't tell what's you and what's the chemical urge of your brain. Or else those are the same thing, and I've been thinking that the vessel is what I am, when really, it's the liquid inside, the muck, which never had a shape to begin with. I looked down to the ground below.

The ghosts were there, all of them, the ones I knew from the store, the ones who hung around the gas station and the mini golf course, the few who lingered outside the motel. They were there, and they were looking up at me. I could see them clear as day, and I loved them all in turn. Spence was shouting something but I was drunk and the wind whipped my hair and I couldn't make out what it was she was trying to get at with language besides she was afraid for me, for what I might do to her if I didn't turn around and come back, and for what I might do to her if I did. That's empathy, or something like it. The ghosts all saw me, and though their faces were wearing the same blank expression they seemed happy to see me, and I smiled down at them and thought I might try to wave.

If I fell, could they catch me? Would they even try?

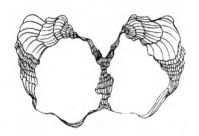

He showed it first to another boy at school—sprouting from the crease in his palm, a little leaf, a three-petaled flower. Of course the other boy tried to pluck it. After all just a boy. He snatched himself away, cradling the bloom like you might a flame in the wind.

He kept it hidden at home, the way little boys of his age start to keep secrets. Locked doors and huffing descended on the household, hugs slid out from under. The twisting embarrassment for the fact of having a mother full up with love for him. A life is unique every time it happens. This much he was sure of.

The way of a secret is to grow, so it was only some weeks before there was no hiding it. The bloom snaked around his forearm and burst open at the elbow, a many-petaled chrysanthemumming starburst of a blossom.

What else: they tried to kill him. They pinned him to the floor and pummeled his kidneys. They knocked him to the ground in the halls and shin-kicked him under lunch tables. They arm-locked him and dug into the skin at the root and tried to pull the plant out by its fleshy plug, but it wouldn't come. It had grown up and in. It felt to the boy like they were pulling on a wire connected to the surest parts of him. It felt awful. He doubled over as they pulled, puppeteered.

He was taken out of school. The isolation made his difference bigger. He cried alone in his room while the vine of himself wrapped up his arm, thick with leaves now, become tougher now, become fibrous, pliant, woodish.

You cannot hide a boy, a body, forever. A body is always pointed toward the world. He craved something not his home. Finally, his mother relented.

They found him, of course, and chased him through the suburbs, and as he was running from them his sprout snagged on a wrought-iron fence, wheeling him around and toppling him. He cracked his head on the brickwork. The boys ran off. The blood pooled, a blood that slicked and spread, that kept coming, that was nothing magic, that didn't even have the decency to mean something.

LETTER HOME

There's not much to build a person with up here. No mud or clay or old newspapers to stuff into a shirt. I can't get one of your ribs either, ha ha. I know you'll probably see this as a betrayal at first, just like you see so much of what I do as betrayal. Maybe that's just what it means to be an astronaut, a wife.

I hope one day you'll forgive me, or at least admire the amount of creativity and belief it took to make my doppleganger. I started with an old flight suit, one that had been stained when a food pouch burst. In the center, I crumpled up a picture of you. Old mission logs, manuals that we didn't need except as a totem against the kind of emergencies we wouldn't survive anyway. When the decommissioning of the station picked up and we started packing up the tools, I would slip away with one, to give the new me form, structure. Socket wrench for shoulder. A screwdriver to give the foot its shape. Things like that.

The hair I needed was easy. You just had to know where to look. Every nook and cranny of the space station holds secrets, especially after all these years. People are so used to looking at the floor for dirt. Even those of us who have been here forever tend to look down when they can't find their pen. I remember how you used to lose things almost immediately, and you would spin a circle to see where you'd set down the Windex or your fork. It was charming, once. And still.

In some ways it was a half-serious project, just a way to pass the time while we counted down the days to our flight home. Maybe I was doing it so that you could see how similar we are, how we're both so engaged in the act of making ourselves. But also I was doing it as an escape from the reality of coming home. I miss you, still. I'm dead homesick if you have to know.

But the view of Earth from the window. The feeling of it. We are all small, and up here, we are smaller. I don't think I can bear again to be sitting at a coffee shop and seeing some cat-struck bird, missing one foot at the ankle. Just the awful futile suffering of it. I can't bear to be within a context. The dread I've often felt of expectation, of being pleasing or not pleasing, both of which are the same burden. And I know this sounds a little like it is about you or the weaknesses of our marriage, but you'll have to take me at my word that it's not.

She was finished with about a week left before the shuttle was set to dock and take us home. A little ratty, yes, but a good enough likeness, especially since I myself have grown more than a little ratty. Only the Russians noticed the switch when I made it. They would look at the real me like I had gone crazy whenever I placed the new me wherever I was supposed to be, posed her in a drifting version of whatever I was supposed to be doing. I would smile at them as though it were a prank and go back to my little sleep area. The American astronauts were happy to oblige the change. Captain Garrett, you'll remember, always found me too willful, anyway. That ol' boys club, NASA. I'd made him the perfect woman.

I know what I'm doing, staying up here. I know that they're going to crash the space station into the Pacific, and if my plan works, I'll still be here when it happens. And that's okay. I need you to know that it's okay. Because when I got up here, and I saw, it was like I could feel all the sinews and the strings that tethered me to that heavy burden I've always had inside slowly pulling taut and snapping. Up here, there's nothing, and you're even part of it a little bit. Isn't that nice?

I'm putting this note in her pocket in the hope that you're

the only one that will find it. Treat her kindly, as she's somewhat poorly made. Whatever you do, try not to assign her too much meaning. Bury her if you feel it's right, or keep her someplace close, so that you might be reminded of a freer me.

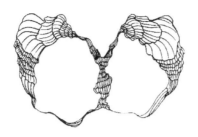

*The bird looked just like her ex-husband, so she hated it.
It was a productive hate. She would arrive home from work
and find the bird still there in the living room, which contained
the TV but also the bird's brass cage and its newspaper
shittings and its beaked, judging face. So: she avoided the
living room, spent her evenings instead tending to a garden,
organizing a basement, or downing a bottle of wine in the
woods behind her house. She loved a good project.*

*She had bought the little cage because she liked the
tarnished look of it, thought it would make for good knick-
knackery. She was on her own and buying things in order to
be alive in a new kind of way. She doesn't know when the bird
arrived, just that suddenly there was chirping and a frail little
monster eyeing her in her own home.*

*She did not want to be a bird person and feared she was.
This is one trouble in being alive. She thought herself
intentional, a spreadsheeter, a woman with a five-year plan.
The bird would chirp, and she would wince, a person trapped
inside a context that narrowed and kept narrowing until it
reached an end.*

*She thought to drive a sewing needle into its breast. She
thought to put bird and cage in a gutter. She thought to sell it,
to give it away to the young girl down the street, to shake the
cage until it stopped shaking back, to pickle it and prepare it
the way the French used to do, ortolan, a meal that supposedly
God himself despised, not that God had bothered much with*

her. The bird sat there on a perch regarding her with one eye, and she didn't do any of these things. She fed it more seed and bought it a little mirror, hoping it would stop looking at her. It didn't.

REMAINDERS

There was this awful thing that happened: a passenger plane had a catastrophic failure. An engine caught fire and went all to shrapnel. The fuselage ripped wide, the only warning the ding of the seatbelt sign moments before. Here's the miracle: the plane landed, and many lives were saved. Though, of course, some were not saved. That's definitely worth remembering when you see the pilot being interviewed on the news. Sure, he's a hero, with a hero's demeanor and a hero's neat, professional moustache, but what of all those tumbledown stories cut short? What of the precious dead?

Point is: one of the not saved landed in my backyard. I saw him there, face-down, half in my garden. He'd smashed my tomato plants all to hell. And I loved those plants. I'd even bought a pellet gun just to shoo the squirrels off of them. I'm a frugal person and a pacifist, so you can see that the plants mattered to me.

At first I thought he was some blackout drunk who'd not made the full trek from the bars back to fraternity row. My house was between the two, which I was reminded of every Thursday, Friday, and Saturday night after last call. Though I'd been one of those kids not long before, their existence had begun to make me unreasonably angry. I saw the cliché of it, too, which gave that anger a bitterness and a meta element, like I was also angry that I had become so invested in this nasty kind of stand-your-ground, get-off-my-lawn nonsense when not long ago I'd sat in a class half-stoned really *getting* that one Robert Frost poem about fences.

I grabbed my pellet gun to sort of scare him and stormed over there, shouting out *Hey asshole* as I went in my sternest homeowner voice. Of course, he was beyond being scared by then, and I was too shocked by the sight of him up close to feel foolish about yelling at a dead man. He was heavyset and middle-aged. I remember he was wearing fun socks. His shoes were gone. The socks had Bigfoot on them, doing that hunched walk from the famous blurry photo.

It was a late Saturday morning. I don't habitually watch the news, so to me this was some kind of miracle or else a horrible omen. I looked up to the cloudless sky, the sun painfully bright above me. I don't know what I was looking for. Some fireball, a hot air balloon, something to offer up explanation. But there was nothing. It was just me in my yard standing over Bigfoot, another one of life's mysteries that wouldn't unravel.

A crow landed on my fence and cawed. It startled me. "Beat it," I said. The crow gave me some side-eyed menace. I pumped the lever on my pellet gun a few times, and it flew off. My ankles cracked when I knelt down over Bigfoot. Sweat tickled my side. If I left him out here, things could get bad. If I brought him inside... well, could I even bring him inside? I didn't mean from an ethics perspective. I meant could I even get the thing done. It seemed like one of those jobs that would be easy in practice but quickly went to pieces once you were doing the actual work. My ambition to tackle projects far exceeds my ability. I've got a half-finished coffee table in my garage that proves that point pretty well. Still, I had to do something.

I stood up and had a little think, which got me around to why I'd come out back in the first place. The marijuana plants by my back fence looked a little wilted in the sun but otherwise were coming along fine. They needed water. I weighed my whiteness, my university job, my clean-cut look against the police being in my backyard and their willingness to let a thing like this go. The plants had grown well, and I'd not paid attention to how big they'd gotten, as my neighbors were cool and one of them was actually looking to buy some of the harvest. I'd started it mostly as a hobby, just a little bit of DIY nonsense from a guy who grows veggies and can bake his own bread. It was probably a felony amount at this point.

I had what felt like a very lucid thought standing there with a pellet gun dangling at the end of my arm, my back to the man: *You are in shock and are therefore concerning yourself with the more mundane aspects of your yard.* It seemed true enough. Meanwhile the sun was so bright, and bright is heat, and et cetera. My next thought was *Dig up the plants and bag them and put the bags in the dumpster down the road and call the police.* But then I thought of me not getting it all, of a K9 unit coming to search my yard for some identifying clue and finding some stray root or leaf. And even if that didn't happen, I thought of all the ways I might be guilty of something. I'd had a fear of trouble instilled in me from a very young age.

All of this was terrible—there was no clean way out of it. I was a rebel in principle, but my clothes were all from Old Navy. My record was spotless.

I went back to the man and squatted over him. "I can't let you do this to me," I said. Bigfoot did not protest.

He wasn't wearing a ring, he didn't have a wallet bulging from his back pocket. A tomato plant looked as though it was growing bent out of his armpit. I'm not much for religion, but I still believe we've all got some sin. Bigfoot too. I felt craven, but he was going to ruin my life. I had to get him out of sight and then gone. I knew of a place, a few miles from town. It was a turnoff to an abandoned farm that ran near to a hiking trail, and people came along often enough trying to get laid or high or both that he'd only be there a day or two before being found. All I had to do was get him there.

I went around the side of my house, where a wheelbarrow full of mulch was still sitting from the early spring. It had sunk into the ground some from a series of hard rains. The mulch had a patchy fur of mold all over it. I kicked the wheelbarrow onto its side then shook as much of the mulch out as I could. The hose was all unraveled and kinked, so I had to straighten it out to get any pressure to rinse out the wheelbarrow clean enough. After, I took the time to put the hose in neat loops on its rack.

There was a haphazard stack of old towels on the shelf over the washer, which was right inside my back door. I grabbed them all, used one to dry out the wheelbarrow, then spread the rest out in it to make a sort of pallet. The man was beyond comfort, but I still felt it was worth doing.

His body was intact, though he looked a little loose and unstructured. I rolled him over and positioned the wheelbarrow behind his head. My thinking was I would pick him up by his shoulders and walk backwards straddling the bowl of the wheelbarrow. He looked to be about two-hundred pounds. It seemed mostly doable.

His face had turned purple from the impact and from the blood pooling. I thought of the blood in my veins, how it fights gravity all day, each heartbeat an act of defiance against the planet's pull. There in his face was the end of the war. If I'd let myself think on it instead of on the next steps I needed to take, it would've broken my heart.

I got down by him and got him under the arms as planned. He smelled like I did after going on a run, mammalian and salty. His belly was taut when I brushed it, and his arms were loose in their sockets. He was impossibly heavy. I walked backward and bumped the wheelbarrow and the whole operation collapsed on top of itself with me in the middle.

I rolled him off of me and realized I was crying. It was very selfish crying, like, it was a *There's no happy way out of this* kind of cry. We lay like that awhile. It smelled like tomato plants and mulchy earth and a little of blood. I'd cut myself on the bent tomato cage. Not badly, but enough to be alarmed. There was tetanus to think of. I felt close to Bigfoot, like we had a shared plight. Neither of us was getting out of this unscathed. This plan would end in failure, and I needed a new one.

Later, once I found out where he'd come from, I'd feel a profound connection. He was one of twelve casualties. The religious significance of the number did not escape me. The news didn't release photos or names. I couldn't bear to go looking for them either. I was too much a coward, too worried about browser histories and my mental health. He just became Bigfoot, my lost disciple, the guy I buried under my vegetable garden. Proof that the world is cruel and strange.

I reached over and put my hand on top of his, wrapped it up in mine. We were two lost travelers, the remainders of a story. The parts that don't line up quite right, the parts with no poetry or broader meaning—a life cut short, one careening on. Doesn't matter which is which.

Did he choose where to land? Did he look down on my garden, and, for a brief moment of lucidity outside of the terror of knowledge, think to himself, *There*?

Of course not, but also: there's no way of knowing what the dead are thinking. After a moment, I resigned myself to what came next. I stood up and got him around the chest again, pulled him to the side of the yard, where the fence would shade him for a few hours yet. I covered him with the towels. I did what I could to prepare him a place where he'd not be forgotten. I dug out the whole garden for him. It was simple work until it wasn't, until my knees jellied and fire shot up my arms and into my spinal cord with each shovelful. My body said enough, and I kept on. In this way I made his last wish for him, pretending it wasn't my own: a good home, a good use, a way to maybe carry on. And the next season my harvest would be greater than it had been, and he would be back in my mind after I was almost able to forget, and every season after I would stand in my backyard and the garden would look as though it was bursting forth with jewels, with all of that beauty that comes later, after the work is done.

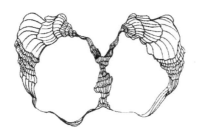

His job was lopping off heads. Fuck, it was so boring. Fuck, he couldn't bear another head rolling just right and looking up at him, eyes already dead, fuck. He would bring his axe down and fuck, every time, fuck. Sometimes a head would spout and spout and it was like fuck, I am just trying to earn a living and maybe provide for a family someday. Meanwhile he had all this red on him that wouldn't wash out. It always found its way down the front of his thick apron, clotted up in his arm hair. No matter how much he showered, he'd find some on his day off—in the bellybutton, tucked behind an ear, crusted into the fold of a toe or embedded too deep under a nail or one time a drop of it dried rust-red on the tip of his member. How the blood got where it got, he never quite knew.

Even being the best employee at the beheadery, even being very good at it, wasn't enough for him, though he knew it was honest work, and needed doing, and doing well. There is unkindness in an unsteady swipe, there is jaggedness and a gasping sound that doesn't go away after it is silent. He won a plaque for himself at the employee picnic, but he couldn't bear to put it in a plaque place like the mantle or his home office. He kept sharp things from his home, lived on takeout so he didn't have to chop anything. And he pined. He pined for something or someone he didn't even have a concept of.

Once, when he was getting pizza with a woman named Joan, he saw the man behind the counter stretching the dough, tossing it, dusting the counter and placing it down, laying out the sauce with a ladle, spreading the cheese in one motion, dotting the pie with goodness in the way of onion and sausage and mushroom, doing something real, something matterful, with tenderness. The man making pizza was so good that it was automatic and beautiful, and watching it happen the head-lopper thought that's me. I'm gorgeous like that. He turned to Joan and thought he might be able to fall in love with her. They smiled at each other, and he thought to tell her how much the man making pizza had moved him.

She scrunched up, then, and leaned forward. She reached out with her hand, and with a fingernail scraped a dry bit of blood from his face, reminding him: he was and ever would be himself.

YOUR BEST SELF

My first class started out in a standoff with an inanimate object. The overhead screen kept rolling back up whenever I let go. It sounded violent, like a ripcord, like Tom Cruise falling down the side of a building. I felt precisely twenty-seven years old standing in front of a group of fifth graders who didn't respect my tie, very unqualified, my truest self.

"You can't do this to me," I said, quietly, to the overhead screen. "I have a syllabus."

Grace Atkins was watching from the narrow rectangle of a window in the door. I smiled at her, let go of the overhead and stage-shrugged as it flapped its way up the wall. She came in then and showed me the trick to keeping it down, which required a flick of the wrist. Honestly, it was a little sexy. I wanted to tell her that she'd be good at riding horses, but my mouth went dry and I thought she would know what I sort of really meant and there were also the kids to consider, who hadn't settled down but seemed to be generally aware of everything that was going on anyway. A few of them were looking at me intently, trying to figure me out.

Grace Atkins was shorter than me and had her hair back and was wearing a shirt that, up close, was actually patterned with birds and foxes, not the floral pattern I'd assumed from the parking lot that morning.

"There you go," she said. "I'll be across the hall if anything else proves too difficult for you." It was a joke that I could tell she meant to be mean-spirited and condescending but maybe didn't have the heart to commit to. She was decidedly not flirting.

Could I say the thing about horses? I could not. Could I?

I said the thing about horses. The kids snickered. Grace

made a face that was politely disgusted and left me alone with them.

For three days, we sat in silence doing various worksheets I had found in a drawer and photocopied for them. My predecessor had a fondness for diagramming sentences. The kids were all pretty quick except for Charlie Humphrey—they blew through the drawer's offerings and then sat doodling and getting restless while Charlie sat in the back writing *gerund* for every word he didn't know. On the fourth day, the only thing left in my predecessor's drawer was some junk mail and a copy of an I-9 tax form, so I photocopied those and had the students diagram those sentences too. When Matthew Plotz raised his hand and whined, "Mr. Bridges, can we maybe diagram some interesting sentences," I said, "Sure thing, Matty."

I went to the white board and wrote, "With malicious intent, Matthew began to question the pedagogical philosophy of his betters, resulting in his expulsion from the charter school and eventual addiction to alcohol and prescription painkillers; however, he was able to make a decent living satisfying the peccadilloes of certain older gentlemen."

Plotz sunk into his chair and sulked. Lucy Green's hand shot right up, and I ignored it. She sat there for the rest of the period, arm rod-straight, hand gone limp at the top of it, a marionette with all but one string cut. I admired her dedication.

Judging by my students' work, federal tax forms have sentences that are startling in their complexity, though who knows if the kids are correct. I wasn't one for grammar. The students believed me when I said I was using a new, gradeless teaching philosophy. The students believed most anything. Occasionally, I would see Grace Atkins at the window, and I would smile with feigned nonchalance and try not to think of our having sex in my car. I had been unhappy in life for some time, which I used to justify her objectification. I know that's a poor excuse.

The principal caught me by the arm in the hallway while I was headed to my car. He was a real name-abbreviator. He said, "Can I borrow you for a second, Bry?"

"Sure thing." We stood facing down the empty hall. I jammed my free hand into my pants pocket. Whenever I talked to an adult man, I felt like I was in trouble, regardless of context. I also suspected that he knew I was here because the money was livable and most of my other options had been snuffed out, either by the suffocating job market or my own lack of ambition.

"I just wanted to remind you that the kids at this school are special."

"Yeah, I know. They've been a real pleasure so far."

He gripped my arm tighter and wheeled himself in front of me, a smile tense and skeletal on his face. "You don't understand."

He had this tight, curly hair that seemed to be thinning out in chunks. I tried to focus on that, on how he looked like the floor of my uncle's basement rec room.

We stood that way for a few seconds, his hot breath mingling with mine. Finally, I said, "You're right, I don't." Grace Atkins walked by without looking at us, her hands full of books and student papers. I called out to her. She flinched but kept walking. The principal put his free hand on my shoulder and squeezed it in a way that he probably felt was paternal but made me keenly aware of my muscle's relatively tenuous relationship with bone.

He smiled. "I just want you to be on your toes. They'll surprise you."

"Sure thing, man." I'd forgotten his name.

He pulled me in for a hug and clapped me hard on the back. From the end of the hallway, Grace looked back before checking the exit door with her body. I couldn't see the look on her face for all the evening light.

We had a pop quiz where I would put a math problem on the board and call on the kids. It was mostly to see if I knew all their names yet. After the first kid got a question right, I mistakenly said, "You get an A."

Vinay, who was a snotty little dude who I felt bad about hating on account of his pudginess and his ethnicity, whined, "I thought we weren't getting grades," and flopped back in his chair.

"I might give a grade here and there," I said. "But grades are just ephemera, as are all things. Even when someone writes something down and hands it to you, it's nearly already gone."

The kids stared at me. I rolled up my shirt sleeve.

"When I got this tattoo, my girlfriend warned me it was permanent. But it's no more permanent than I am. And she's left, by the way. And I'm rotting away right here in front of you. And you're starting to rot, too."

Vinay busied himself at tying his shoes.

"What is that?" Charlie Humphrey asked. He was a few

rows back and had recently broken his glasses.

"It's a big-ass pair of scissors." I flexed my bicep for them. The class was silent.

"What I mean is that you're all going to die someday," I said. "Worrying about grades is pointless."

One of the kids looked like she might cry. Vinay got his shoes tied, scowled, and yanked the laces free again.

Weeks went by. The kids sputtered. I ran out of ideas. We sat in frustrated silence. Group work was assigned. Someone punched Billy Emberly hard in the arm, and I assigned different groups.

While we were studying slam poetry, Kelly Lewandowski—Boy Kelly, I called him—stood up on his desk and exclaimed, "I didn't know I hated this / but I do. / I'll always hate it, / like I hate you." The kids who could snap their fingers snapped their fingers.

I stopped Grace before she left her classroom. "How do you keep up momentum?"

She looked at me like I had a turd in my hand. Then she sighed and said, "You have to meet them on their terms. What you care about isn't necessarily what they care about."

"Yeah, but what do they care about?"

"They're kids. They care about kid stuff."

I had no idea at all what that might be.

She was ready to be finished talking to me, but I was standing in the doorway. She looked at the stuff on her desk, riffled some papers. When she looked back up at me, she saw the lost look on my face. I doubled down on looking sad, shuffled a foot. She wasn't the type to kick a sack of kittens in the river.

"Just," she stopped to gather up her belongings, making it clear we were about to be done. "Just be real with them. They're people. If you treat them like that, they'll jump on board."

"Be real with them."

"That's it."

"I can do that."

Plotz was wearing a shirt that said "FUCK COPS," like that, all caps. Apparently something had happened downtown. I don't watch the news. Plotz was too young to distrust the police, so I figured his parents were probably activists of some kind, which I respected from a distance. But also: you don't see nice cops hanging around schools and being friendly like they used to during the D.A.R.E. program days. Now they were uniformed bullies, same as any other. But also also: these were healthy, mostly white children in a rich part of town whose parents were paying too much money for a charter school because homeschooling was outside the bounds of their ability to nurture effectively. They lived devoid of context and pain. We all knew it. The teachers' lounge stank of that knowledge.

I was almost offended. Not for the swear word, and not for the cops, because of course fuck cops. I was offended for the people who had actual cause to say fuck cops.

I set my jaw and said, "'Fuck cops' is not Che Guevara. You can't just put it on a t-shirt."

Billy Emberly's hand shot up.

"What, Billy?"

"Who's Shea Guevera?"

Had I said Shea? I felt a little mushmouthed all the time

lately. If I could, I would dismiss them and go stare at my tongue in the bathroom mirror, but I was stuck here with them.

"*Che* Guevera is a famous revolutionary."

The little buck-toothed one (Cheryl? Charlotte?) put her hand up and said, "If he's famous, why don't we know him?"

I didn't have it in me to explain. Explaining might lead to more questions, ones I couldn't answer. Like: what country did he revolutionize? What happened to him? My knowledge of the man sort of began and ended with my junior-high fondness for Kurt Cobain.

"Because of the cops," I said, finally, and then, because I saw no other way out, I led them in a rousing chant of "Fuck the police" before we spent the afternoon watching bleeped out NWA songs on Youtube. I caught Grace through the window, looking exasperated, but the joy in the room was infectious, and I smiled, and then I turned back to her while the kids sang along.

Grace broke a heel in the parking lot while I was walking up behind her. Her ankle rolled a little, and she stumbled. She took the shoe off and stared at the limp heel. "Fu—Fudge everything," she said. Kids were starting to arrive.

As I caught up to her, she looked like she might fall over, since she was standing like a flamingo on crumbling asphalt. I took it upon myself to steady her by putting a hand on her arm, and she tensed up. "Jesus Christ, you scared me."

"Sorry. I was just trying to help. Do you need a shoe?"

She glared up at me. "Do you *have* a shoe?"

I shrugged. "I do not."

She shook my hand off, saying. "Let's get something clear

here. I don't like you. I'm not going to like you. This isn't a meet-cute. The kids might not see through you, and the principal might not see through you, but I do. You're all razzle, no dazzle. So leave it be, buster."

Probably I couldn't help it: I grinned big and a little embarrassed and said, "I like that you called me buster."

She jabbed me in the chest with the toe of her shoe. "Fuck off, buster."

In one motion, she snapped the heel off and dropped it at my feet, then wobbled off in a huff. I knew clear enough I was an idiot and a bad person. What I needed was some way to make her see past my veneer of marginal competence to the frail, lovable boy beneath it, if there was one.

I called the children into a huddle and said that we would be trying something new, something we had to keep a secret. Their hands shot up, and I shushed them.

"What we're going to do," I said, "is a little bit of nontraditional education."

Lucy Green's hand stayed up.

"What I mean by that," I said, glaring at Lucy until she put her hand down, "is instead of thinking about normal subjects like math or English, instead of reading *The Phantom Tollbooth* like we were going to this week, we're going to work on becoming our best selves. Everything is bad. As a culture we've blown it. And you. You're special. Everyone tells you so. You shouldn't get to my age and realize you're not who you want to be. So, I want you to take today and think on what you want to really do with your life, and we'll get started on that."

I organized the children into groups of two to four, based

on what they wanted and what I thought they would be best at, and we spent a week arranged this way, with them working on individual projects and helping each other along. Charlie Humphrey was writing out all the uses he could think of for a cashew, since peanuts were already spoken for. So far his list said *1. Eat them. 2. Cashew butter. 3. Shaped like a kidney? 4. Milk?!* Charlie was a bit of a disappointment to me. So, too, were the children trying to find narrative elements in the fascicles of Emily Dickinson. Their readings were pedestrian and uninspired.

I had better students. Billy Emberly invented a pretty good board game called *OrkWarz*. Allen and Sheila developed a disturbing, accurate depiction of dog behavior, such that I had to finally separate them and considered sending Allen home with a note to his mother. Boy Kelly mastered the knife game from the movie *Aliens*, which I had shown him on Youtube. Plotz had his nunchaku. The buck-toothed one (Cherry?) was predicting dice throws using a new property of prime numbers she'd discovered. Vinay ate soap and taught himself to like it. Lucy Green had her crying softly and threatening to tell on everyone, which she was quite good at. John Paul kept finding lizards in interesting places. Overall, it was a good week. For homework I told them to act normal, to sit quietly in their homes and be good children. I told them that they were almost pubescent now, so if anyone asked about what they did at school, they could get away with saying *Nothing* or *God mom* or *Like, math and stuff*. Always say math, I told them. Parents are awed and impressed by math but afraid to reveal how little they know of it, so they'll take you at your word.

. . .

"People are going to look down on this if we let them. What we need if we're really going to become our best selves," I said to the kids, who had all gathered again in a huddle at my desk, "is a lookout."

Things were escalating.

I pointed at the little rectangle window in the door. Plotz nodded solemnly.

"I'm asking for volunteers. I'm asking for people who are solid liars, or who can blend into an environment without being noticed. I'm asking for people who are known for frequent trips to the bathroom and nerves of pure steel. Knowing various bird calls might help."

Lucy Green's hand shot up.

"I'm asking," I said, staring her down, "for people who are unafraid of bucking the system when the system is against them."

Lucy kept her hand up.

"Is that really you, Lucy?"

She shook her head no, but she couldn't help herself. Her hand stayed in the air.

"Everyone in this room loves you, Lucy," I said, patting her on the head, "but out there, there would be a reckoning. I believed you this morning when you swore the Oath of Becoming Our Best Selves together. I believe you now. But out there, you'd betray us all. I don't want that. No one does."

Her chapped lip was quivering, her hand starting to wilt back down to her side.

"It's okay," I said. "Your Best Self is in here, with us."

She was just barely not crying.

"Do you want to go to the Crying Corner for a minute?"

She did.

"It's alright. Go on."

She ran off to the corner of the room we'd covered in black construction paper. Plotz, Vinay, and the buck-toothed one (Cherise?) volunteered to rotate as our lookouts. I sent the rest back to their lessons, which today revolved around learning what a quadratic equation was and whether it was actually of use to us in the modern world, like math teachers always insisted, and if so, how to deploy it in ways that might destabilize neoliberal capitalism. I spent the rest of the afternoon drilling my lookouts on what to say if they were cornered, how to set noise traps, and the various codes they were to text me on the burner phones I'd bought them. They listened, intent and solemn. I was important to them. I was cool.

A physics experiment got out of hand and I had to bury the Harris The Guinea Pig, who was actually a turtle. I couldn't tell if the kids were being clever or if perhaps there once had been a rodent in the cage. A little plaque on the cage said "Harris the Guinea Pig." There was no telling when it was put up, or when the turtle arrived, or if there was some previous tragedy I wasn't privy to. The turtle was definitely dead, though.

"Can we crack him open?" Plotz asked.

"Absolutely not," I said.

Lucy looked upset. It was her miniature cannonball that had done the deed.

"But what's under his shell?"

"Nothing. More turtle."

Plotz sulked. After the funeral, which we had outside under the elm tree, I came across him drawing a broken-open shell with gold coins spilling everywhere. When he looked up at me, he had tears in his eyes. It was a hard day for all of us. I palmed his head like a basketball and turned it away from me.

The image stuck with me though. Once the kids went home, I got the shovel from the maintenance closet and went back under the elm tree, which I saw now was littered with small mounds of earth, dozens of them at least.

Grace was walking through the parking lot. She called out to me, "What are you doing?"

I shrugged and held the shovel. She walked over and pointed at the ground.

"We take the markers down on Fridays. The kids forget."

"Then what happens?"

Grace scowled at me. "The standardized tests are in March. You know we're not exempt from that, right?"

I got the feeling we weren't talking about the same thing. She had some lipstick on her teeth. I really really wanted to have sex with her. Without the kids around, it seemed more appropriate.

I turned and dug in with the shovel. It only took two or three shovelfuls to unearth the shoebox. When I opened it, Grace was gone, and Harris the Guinea Pig was looking up at me, blinking his dopey lids, as alive as he was that morning. I picked him up and shook him a little. He sounded just like a coin purse.

The principal came to my room for a teaching observation. After thinking on it I did my teaching routine as usual. We had a long freewheeler about the Hegelian dialectic, modern practices of dentistry and their partial blame for the oncoming ecological catastrophe, and the phenomenological ramifications of colorblindness. The principal sat in the back of the room in a desk that was too short for his lank. All day he watched me, smiling. He clapped his hands. He said, "Oh, that's good." Everything I did was *marvelous* or *fantastic*.

At the end of the day he told me: I'm doing great. He told me: the kids love me. He told me: he's getting a divorce, and it's been hard. He told me: he's worried he might have hypothyroidism. He told me: I look like that one guy from that movie, I know the one. He told me: he was born without a pinky toe on his left foot and that for a long time he was prone to falling over. He told me: he hopes I'm not *lack toes intolerant*. He told me about a timeshare opportunity in Destin, Florida. He told me something else. The gist of the conversation was that I am a very good boy.

I would feel proud of myself if I weren't still thoroughly myself.

Charley Humphrey came up to me looking very serious. "I made a mistake," he said.

I looked up from my phone. "What kind?"

He stood there rod-straight. Then he threw up on my desk, my shirt, and into my lap. An absurd amount of vomit, and it was gray. He ran from me, hands over his mouth, and spewed again over the potatoes that were suspended by toothpicks in their mason jars. The kids were laughing and gasping, and Lucy quietly opened her desk and vomited into it.

Becoming our Best Selves was not going very well. For the rest of the day, I found Charlie's gray vomit in new places.

The lookouts all got detention for a week after Plotz and Vinay were caught in the back seat of the principal's car with a recording device. We abandoned the idea. I told them it was no longer necessary so that I didn't have to tell them it was a misjudgment from the start. I gave them all stickers that said "Mission Accomplished."

Plotz put his sticker on his thumb and waved it inches from my face. "Does this mean I'm my Best Self?"

"No," I said. "That takes a lifetime. Maybe longer."

"Okay," he said, and ran full-tilt to the back of the room, where the other kids were making a zine about the Nietzschean undertones of videogame protagonists. He fell down in the middle of them and shouted, "HE SAID IT WILL TAKE A LIFETIME." There was some grumbling, some trips to the Crying Corner, but before long they got back to work. The zine had a point to make, and they were determined to make it. I admired their dedication, their belief in something that wasn't futile.

Grace Atkins' face framed in the window, looking in suspiciously. Grace Atkins stirring tea and frowning over the dirty mugs in the breakroom sink. Grace Atkins with one arm against the wall, one leg off the ground, putting her pink kitten heel back on after catching it on a rip in the hall carpet. And who wears shoes like that to teach in? Grace Atkins reading aloud to the younger kids in the library while I walked by, staring me down without losing her place in *Hop on Pop*. I might could die from anything at all. Grace too. I pictured her regretting at my funeral. I pictured me dead and splayed out in front of the whole solemn school. The thought followed me into the bathroom, followed me home at night, snuggled up with me in bed. I only put it away in front of the students, and then not entirely.

We were playing a game called *Everything is Philosophy*. The kids liked it. It involved them asking whatever question popped into their heads and my answering it with the first thing that popped into mine.

"Does my cat love me?"

"Your cat's brain is made up of nerve endings that experience electrochemical reactions, same as everything. That it loves you is irrelevant. It *reacts* to you."

"If an airplane was on a conveyer belt, could it take off?"

"Yes. Or maybe not."

"Was Harris traumatized when you buried him alive?"

"We both were."

"How come when there's a bug in the car while the car is driving, the bug doesn't fly backwards relative to the vehicle's motion?"

"..."

"You didn't answer."

"You're not playing the game right."

"What's a dildo?"

"Who's asking?"

"I am."

"I mean where did you hear it?"

"Sunday school."

"It's a church word. Ask someone at church."

Plotz raised his hand. "Am I on fire?"

"No, Plotz."

Plotz looked incredulous. Vinay snapped his fingers and a flame appeared. He'd been studying magic tricks. He raised his hand.

"Yes, you're on fire. Plotz isn't."

The other kids started snapping fingers. I had a headache.

"Everybody cut it out. Vinay, the sprinklers are gonna go off."

The kids all groaned. Charlie Humphrey picked his nose in the Crying Corner.

Grace and I were leaving our classrooms at the same time. I'd made sure of it.

"How'd it go today?" I asked. She shrugged.

"Are you doing anything this weekend?" I asked.

"No." We walked. I kept pace with her. She had a Sorkin-esque walk, harried and heel-clacky. A confident walk, and she spent her day with 8-year-olds. Other people were such ongoing mysteries.

I looked over. Her shirt collar was jouncing with each vigorous step, exposing a collarbone, the pale vulnerability of cleavage. She smelled like vanilla hand lotion, and there was a little bit of damp on her shirt at the armpit. She was looking through a stack of student worksheets and walking fast, and I realized I was veering toward her, that we were about to bump into each other and send her worksheets tumbling, and she would most likely hate me for it and for the cliché of the attempt and for my being generally a skeezer. And: she'd be right to hate me. I kept trying to make her mean something. I kept veering.

Vinay had written a play called *The Artificial Art Official,* and my class was putting it on. It was about a person who didn't know anything about art who kept getting phone calls from art collectors because his name was very similar to a real art critic's. In the play, the main character becomes more and more respected until it all comes crashing down as the world realizes that art is fundamentally meaningless except for the meaning we put on it. I thought it was a little too precious, and I was pretty sure the title had already been done, but I didn't have the heart to tell him so.

Rehearsals had been a mess. The orgy scene was, thankfully, jumbled and unrealistic, though I worried that Charlotte (Charli? Like with an i?) snorting powdered sugar off of a mirror over and over as we tried to get it right was having a real effect on her personality. When I talked to her, she kept trying to look around me at the wall. The dialogue was barely coherent, the acting wooden, the fake beards subpar. I was pitching it as outsider art.

On opening night, I happened to sit next to Grace Atkins. She had brought a very dense-looking man. Not dense as in stupid. Dense as in he had a substantial, adult body and looked good in a fitted shirt. I found myself downplaying the production to him, saying things like *They're going to just do their best* and *I try to be supportive*. He nodded, and he nodded. No one got punched in the jaw.

The audience was rapt. I fidgeted in my chair as Boy Kelly flubbed lines and the sword fight degenerated into chaos. When Vinay's character was supposed to fly out of the scene, only one wire was reeled in, leaving him dangling horizontally a few feet off stage. It ended to thunderous applause and me quietly sneaking out the side door of the gym to smoke the cigarettes I'd bought.

Sitting on the curb of the parking lot, I reminded myself I did not care at all about any of this.

Grace Atkins and the man she'd brought walked out. I stood up, wiped gravel off my ass.

Grace walked up to me and stuck her hand out. "You owe me one of those."

I gave her one of those. The man got one too. He lit hers with a lighter he had.

She sucked in on the cigarette. "That was a real bad play."

I nodded. She clenched herself at the elbows, dangling her cigarette without care. I kept my eye on it. It was a perfectly good cigarette.

"Well, goodnight," she said, and tucked herself into the man's armpit. The two of them walked off. A rush of children erupted from the clangy doors. They kept coming and coming without end.

Eighteen of my twenty students came in with broken limbs. Arms, wrists, legs. Chemise (?) had her whole torso wrapped up in addition to her arm, which was held out from her body and bent at the elbow. All day I kept asking if she had a question, and she shook her head.

Lucy and Plotz were the only ones unscathed. There were clatters of crutches everywhere in the room. Finally, I called the two of them up to my desk. Plotz tripped over a kid's rigid leg and I winced, expecting him to go down hard and shatter his pelvis. He turned it into a joke, windmilling his arms and pretending to be off-balance. I glowered. He straightened up.

"What happened?" I asked them.

Plotz shrugged. Lucy said, "Mr. Bridges, I'm so sorry."

"It's not your fault, Luce." Her eyes watered.

Plotz started to talk and one of his teeth fell out on my desk. The three of us stared at it.

"Was that a baby tooth?" I asked.

"That was a grown-up tooth," Plotz said, a little blood leaking from his mouth.

I took him across the hall. Grace Atkins' students were all very healthy looking, their bodies whole and belimbed and wispy-haired. They would look great on an old-timey carousel. I looked at Plotz, who had a glob of dry grape jelly on his shirt and his own tooth in hand.

Grace squatted down to look Plotz in the eye. "How did this happen?" She looked up at me with accusation.

I shrugged. "Everybody has a broken bone." Lucy watched from the doorway.

Grace looked back at Plotz. "Matthew, do you need to go to the nurse?"

There was something maternal and sexy about it all. I looked down at Grace's desk. There was a book on it, and on the cover a family of cartoon koalas. The mother was wearing a dress, had a clearly feminine shape. I did not picture the lady koala naked. To do so would be absurd.

"I'll be okay," he said. I knew he didn't mean it.

I said, "Plotz, go to the nurse."

He shook his head.

"Plotz, how are you going to become your Best Self if you've got a hobo's mouth?"

From the doorway, Lucy wailed, "I'm sorry, okay? I'm sorry for what happened!"

Grace looked at me. Her kids watched us, stone-faced. I looked around the room. So many bright-colored words on the wall, and maps, and turkeys drawn from traced hands, and flags of many countries.

"This is a great classroom," I said. I really meant it.

. . .

My class had a new student, and he was wearing the same shirt as I was. It was a bad day for everyone. Billy Emberly wanted to know what was with all the President's Day shit I'd put up on the walls, except he called it Lincoln crud. I called a conference in the hallway with everyone but the new kid.

"Sometimes you have to fit in," I said. Two or three kids started crying.

"Sometimes in order to be your Best Self you have to learn how to assimilate into the system. Sometimes you put a president on the wall, and you decorate valentines and put them in each other's little mailboxes, and you go to college for something that is sort of like what you'd want to do but not precisely it. Sometimes that is your Best Self. That, Billy, is what's with the Lincoln crud."

Vinay and Boy Kelly started muttering to each other in the blood-brother language they'd invented. I know it's just swear words said backwards, but I've been ignoring that. I looked in the window, and the new kid was sitting at his desk, dressed just like me, hands folded over a piece of red construction paper he'd cut into a lopsided heart, weeping openly, his shoulders jumping up and down.

The standardized exams loomed. The principal roamed the halls, jumping back any time someone opened a door in his path, which was frequently. I didn't know what a dervish was or if to call him a whirling one would be cultural appropriation. Anyway he was going bugfuck nuts about the standardized tests.

He pulled me out of class and walked me down to his

office while my students stared at the fat workbooks we'd been given that Monday. "Brian, we have to do well."

"We'll do well."

"Oh thank god. If we don't do well...." He stood up and wandered from the room. I sat there for a minute, and he didn't return. My fart purred into the vinyl office chair while I looked at certificates on the wall. I went back to my classroom.

The kids complained and flopped in their seats. I walked up and down and looked at their work. Most of the spaces were left blank. Most of the paragraphs were uncomprehended. X had not been solved for in any meaningful way. I realized we wouldn't do well.

At the end of the day, I called them all together and gave them an underdogs-in-the-locker-room pep talk you wouldn't believe. I said that things would be fine because that's what we'd call them once we got past this. I told them all they had to do was believe in themselves. I told them that they were on their way to becoming their Best Selves regardless of what happened tomorrow during the exam. I told them that failure was not an ending but a beginning, that most things were a kind of failure with the right perspective, and so when a real failure came along, they only had to remember that it fit right in with everything that had come before. Lucy tried to get people to hold hands. They didn't take her up on it. We had a moment of silence, then I sent them out into the world, my children.

I was sitting in the parking lot drinking beer. It was a Saturday, a special field day for the kids, races, ribbons, that kind. The exams were over, and we were blowing off steam as a school while we waited on results. I watched them from the curb, far enough off that they looked like someone else's problem. I was thinking that there should be more of a plot to my life. I'd been here all year and was in the exact same place. Plotz was next to me swigging on a sports drink. I asked him about it.

"Man, look around," he said.

I asked him what he meant.

"Days go by at this place. That's all it is. It takes a really long time."

He hocked and spat a blue loogie between his legs. We were sitting just the same, legs apart, arms on knees, and he reached over and put a hand on one of my arms.

"Lack of momentum is its own momentum," he said.

The words struck me. I knew already I was a steward to that which doesn't add up to anything. I didn't realize the kids might know it too. That was the way of it, though: I am here, and then I was here, the kids go up a grade and begin the long process of forgetting me in my entirety. And some of them will be their Best Selves, and all of them will be their Best Selves, and Grace will marry someone who is not me while her students pass the standardized tests, and I will leave here to do other, other things. Meanwhile here I was mistakenly clinging to the idea that it had to add up to something. Everything with a fit. Had to. I didn't believe that I believed it, but maybe the way I felt when Plotz put it in my face was the proof that I did. And by believing it, I'd been awful to everyone around me, and I'd justified that awfulness by thinking that I was going somewhere. Sometimes these things just make themselves plain in the end.

"It's never going to work, is it? Being our Best Selves?" Plotz asked.

I shrugged. "It's worth trying."

Plotz hocked another loogie. "You've been jerking us around."

We sat there in silence.

"You're a good kid, Plotz," I said.

"Sure."

Grace was on the field in blue jeans and a free t-shirt from a 5k, refereeing a potato sack race. She hopped alongside the contestants, and when they all collapsed in a heap, she put her hand to her face, probably to cover laughter. The kids were gorgeous, the sun was gorgeous, Grace was gorgeous. I waved at her. She saw me clearly, and she didn't wave back. I told myself I was fine with it. I told myself I'd somehow become my Best Self.

"Try and remember me saying that."

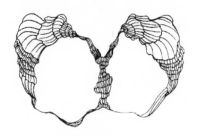

A man came down out of the smoke and lived with us for a time. Something was always on fire, or about to be on fire, or just finished being on fire. It was summer. The man poked around town, bought a few things from the drugstore, set up a little camp in the backfield past where the little leaguers could hit.

At first, we didn't mind him. We didn't wonder where he came from, since we knew: the smoke. It made enough sense at the time. Now we wonder, but that's the way of a now. He would sleep through morning, wake up in the sweaty parts of the day and get gently drunk, hassle the children playing softball with a kind of good humor you don't see much in adult men. We knew he was a threat, but we liked him anyway.

Meanwhile, the smoke moved closer, blanketed the mornings with thick haze, turned the moon to blood when we could see it at all. Our windows were sealed, we were like to bake in our homes. The man grew lonely with us all indoors. That's how it looked, anyway. He wandered from house to house, peering in, knocking loose-knuckled on glass. It was then that we became afraid. Of him, for him. We didn't know.

We wanted him gone. We told him so through cracked windows. We told him it wasn't safe to be here with us. He said we didn't know what we were talking about, or he opened his mouth and no sound came out, and the sound of crackling flames around him went silent, too, or he smiled, orange glinting off the plaque of his teeth, the burning that was coming preambled in the light on his face. King of smoke, ash king, char king, king of burn, king of all of this ending. At the window and happening.

HOUSEWARM

When the truck arrived outside I was home to see it. The truck wasn't marked, but it had that rectangular brown authority to it that kept me at the window to see if I had a package, though I wasn't expecting one. When I was younger, first living on my own, my mother would send a box full of candy and doodads for around the house, proof that she'd been thinking of me. I could look forward, every other month or so, to a continued insistence that I was alive and in some way still hers.

What was in them became erratic as her mind went. When I was in my first apartment, I would get a spatula, a butter dish, a hideous wall-clock, and though our tastes and priorities were becoming so different—I ate out (mostly), I avoided fat (mostly), I had a cell phone to tell the time—the logic to the gifts was clean. Things changed so slowly that by the time I was receiving doll clothes and newspaper clippings, there was no way to figure out where things had begun to go wrong. Then the frequency of them diminished, and then one day the last one came. It was a pipe carved into the shape of a guitar and a religious tract that had been stepped on more than once.

That's not the story I'm telling, not really. It's never the story I'm telling. But maybe you can see why some part of me was eager.

A man in short sleeves and a tie came to me with a clipboard. Asked me to sign, so I did. He nodded and walked back into the door of truck. He appeared again holding three large boxes at once. They blocked his view, and through some awkward maneuvering I held the door open for him. Another truck pulled up as we went inside, looking just the same. I

162

thought it was a strange coincidence or just some lost driver, but he got out with confidence carrying a few boxes of his own.

I followed the first man into my living room. He cut one of the boxes open with a blade and showed me that it was full of hair. I stepped back from him. "What am I supposed to do with this?" I asked. He shrugged. "You signed for it." Then he dumped it out on the rug. The second driver came in with his boxes while the first broke down and flattened the now-empty box. They worked in tandem, dumping hair and stacking up the boxes while the pile grew and started spilling onto the hardwood.

"Please stop." I said.

"Can't." They said. And so it went on. The pile of hair started spilling over itself, making tufts that floated and gusted along the floor. I went to the closet and grabbed a broom, started sweeping it up into one pile, but each time the men would come in with more boxes, hair would flutter away again.

I looked on the paper I'd signed and dialed the phone number. There was no answer, just a beep, so I left a message saying there was some mistake, a clerical error of some kind. I had to stop midway through my sentences to pull hair off my tongue. It was getting into the air, sticking to things, different lengths and colors and textures, head hair and body hair and pubic hair and all of it human most likely. The men brought in more boxes. Behind them, more men had arrived in trucks. They waited outside with still more boxes, standing around on my lawn, smoking and cracking wise.

I went outside and implored them. "There was a clerical error. You've got the wrong guy."

One of them looked at his clipboard and read my name

back to me, my address. I wanted to sit down on the lawn but didn't. A man with too many boxes to see veered close to me, and I stepped aside. He squatted down to fit through the door, but one of the boxes hit the jamb and toppled over anyway.

The men worked unloading the trucks through the afternoon. I stood and watched as my home filled up with hair, as the pile they'd formed in the living room became generally distributed by their efforts. I walked the perimeter of my house, peering into windows. In some rooms it was waist-high already. Still the men came. Another truck pulled up, this one pulling a flatbed laded with tightly rolled bales of hair. A man in the passenger seat had a pitchfork between his legs, its tines jutting out the cab through the rolled-down window.

"What's that for?" I asked, desperate for things to stop, or at least to be understood, but mostly for them to stop.

In reply he feinted at me with the pitchfork and smiled wider than I thought a face could while still staying ugly. Another worker came out huffing and spitting, wiping at his mouth with hair-covered hands. They pulled him aside and had a long, hushed talk. They being the other men, who had become numerous, milling around my yard when they weren't unloading or unpacking. There were too many even to do the job, though the job was substantial and the ones at the boxes were furred with hair and sweat. I watched them, then was startled when a bale rolled off the flatbed behind me. It didn't crash. It made a *fwoomp* sound as it landed and shoved some air toward me. The pitchfork man stood above it on the truck, levering the next bale onto the ground with his tool. It *fwoomped* too. They all did.

Finally, I abandoned my dignity and sat down in my yard like a bored child waiting on his tantrum to arrive. I started picking at the blades of grass, yanking them out at the root. The men stepped over me with their cargo. The lawn was dry and going to yellow—the tops of the blades were already starting to turn. It was summer. In years past, I'd spent my Sundays moving a sprinkler around and running a timer, making sure that I got good coverage over every square inch of green. This year it hadn't seemed to much matter.

I stayed there focused on the grass while the men did their work. The grass had been so supple last year, a deep living green that would spring right back when I walked barefoot to get the paper. I ran my hands over it and found it was stiff, crackly. There seemed no point in fighting what was happening. Something about all this felt earned. Not that I would say so. The men seemed to be enjoying the work, like it wasn't an injustice. They were glad to be doing it. I thought of trying to save my grass if I could.

When the house was full up with hair, the men were all back-slapping each other and hooting. One of them dragged me up off the turf and shook my hand vigorously. His eyes were all wrinkled up on themselves he was smiling so hard. Then they got into their trucks and left, all but the pitchfork man. It was a big production getting everyone turned around in the narrow cul-de-sac, and we both watched it.

The pitchfork man turned to me with a kind of disaffected pity. He said, "Things sure do know how to get worse."

"You did this," I said.

He looked away. "Sun's near down now. You want a drink?"

Before I could answer, he walked to his truck and tossed the pitchfork into the cab. Then he hoisted himself in, got the engine chugging, and looked back at me. When I didn't respond he shrugged and drove off.

I looked back at my house. Someone had yanked up the blinds on all the windows. The hair wasn't packed in as tightly as I'd expected—light still shone out in places.

I walked to the front window and pressed a hand to the glass. A neighbor and his dog stopped to consider me looking in on my own house, then moved on. I heard the A/C click on. The hair began to stir, swirling and dancing over itself, every color of hair catching light and twisting around the other colors. It wasn't anything magic. It was just the air circulating. Still, I liked the way it was moving. I thought of my mother, thought of her being gone. Watching the hair dance and swirl in my living room through the window, it seemed as though if only a meaning could be found, I might be able to enter. I might be able to walk into all that was there and tolerate the itching, the choking dryness of it, and arrive at what was soft and good.

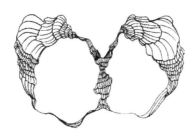

The Rodeo Queen disappeared. This happened during the parade. She felt so wonderful, everyone in town watching, her deer-legged and waving from the back of a Ford Mustang convertible, her still a child but not being treated like a child, she could burst she could burst she could. Then her car at the head of the column turned a corner on the parade route, and she was briefly out of view, and when anyone thought to look at her again, she was no longer there.

An effort was made to locate her. This is what should happen when the Rodeo Queen goes missing. Still, there were calves to rope, and a junior-cowboy costume contest to judge, and an influx of valley people to fit into the town, somehow, and overcharge for parking and places to sleep. The Rodeo King was busy failing biology/masturbating, so he was no help. He had no sense of the mystic or adventure. He just wanted to get by and get on with his life.

What can I say? Sometimes stories don't go anywhere. The Rodeo Queen was there, and then she wasn't. We forgot, quickly and painlessly. She did not get treatment deserving of her status. The world doesn't care about little girls, not really. And if you want this to matter. If you want something real from this. If you want pretty and nice. If you want satisfied. If you want joy. If you want horses barreling in dirt, carving air like there's nothing else but the present and the speed and the insuck of a breath, this one. If you want an answer. If you want something like alive.

ALIGHTING

I woke to Baker in my face, hot-breathing it and doing a yawney whine. I pushed him off my chest, and he stood over me and licked my neck. His muzzle was wet with something thick, sticky. I opened my eyes. The dog's ivory face fur was stained pink with blood, the same shade running up his paws. I scrambled away from him, instinctive, wide-awake and afraid. He backed off, turned a circle, barked twice at me playfully, and went down on his haunches, leaving pink pawprints on my comforter. I felt at my neck, which was slicked with blood-tinged saliva, and then the rest of me, which was mercifully dry and whole.

My sweet boy Baker leaned down and used a back leg to thump at his ear, flecking blood over the room and then sitting there panting. He was fine. So was I. We were both of us animals.

I found my bra tangled in the sheets and tucked it under my arm with my clean hand, then grabbed a pair of shorts and fell into the wall trying to get them on one-handed, leaving a pinkish handprint behind. I tugged down the shirt I'd slept in the past three nights so I could see if there was blood on the collar. There was. I gave up, smeared my hand clean on the shirt, and put the bra on under it.

"Come on, idiot," I said to Baker. "Let's go find your dead mouse."

Baker's ears perked and he hopped from the bed, his nails clacking on the wood as he made his way down the hall. I followed him toward the kitchen. He had done this once before, had left the mouse corpse half-devoured on the kitchen tiles. He was an accomplished spider killer, too, would paw a cockroach or cricket near to shreds. He never ate what he killed, which meant I had to come along later and clean it up.

Except it wasn't any of those things. When I got to the kitchen, I saw Baker sniffing at and then pawing a large bird, gray, its body the length of my forearm. It was splayed and bent on the kitchen floor, one wing underneath it, the short twig legs entangled in each other. It was some kind of parrot, haloed by blood.

I shouted the dog away, and he backed off to where the tile floor of the kitchen met the wood of the dining room. He settled down with his head on his paws, watching me. I went over to the bird.

Its breast was matted with blood. It wasn't the usual round and proud of a bird chest. Probably it was crushed. The bent wing was ripped most of the way free, exposing the tendons underneath the feathers. I knelt down over it, and its good wing fluttered. The bird was alive, still, its breathing ragged, its chest a little broken bellows.

I fell backwards onto the kitchen floor. "Oh, Baker. Oh no."

I had left the kitchen window open the night before. I remembered that before I looked up. The window was screened, though, and the bird had somehow and for some reason forced its way in. The screen was ripped from the corner and tapping against its frame with the breeze.

More than anything, I felt complicit in a crime. Baker shuffled his paws like he might stand up, and I glared at him. I put my hand under the bird's tail and slid it up under its body as gently as I could. The bird fluttered. I pulled it to my chest and stood, not knowing where to put it down or if I should. It turned its head weakly and grabbed onto my thumb with its beak. It dug in with the talons on its unbroken leg. It intended damage, I could tell. Its eye flicked wildly all around, but it was beyond the capacity to do harm.

It let go of me and made a pathetic squawk that gave up midway through. It tried again, and I brought it closer to me, trying to discern if there was anything I could do.

I cradled the bird with one hand, and I held the other palm up under its head. It turned one eye toward me, puffed itself up, and then with the voice of a windup squelching toy said *Where's Jeremy?* and was dead.

After I called in to work, cleaned the floor, washed the dog, and sat staring at the bird wrapped in my bloodied t-shirt inside a shoebox, I tried to think if I knew any Jeremys on this block. I hadn't gotten out much in the year I'd been here, though there had been the usual friendly conversations between my neighbors and me where we introduced ourselves and then realized we hadn't listened closely to the other's name. There were at least two men who might be a Jeremy, but I wouldn't know for sure, and to admit that seemed rude, maybe even cruel, considering the conversation that would follow. Baker sat on a junk towel at my feet, collarless and bath-fluffed and slobbing peanut butter out of a Kong. I couldn't be angry with him for being a dog, but I wanted to be.

I pushed my chair out and stormed off. Baker startled and followed after me for a few steps before returning to his towel. A minute to think would help, a walk around the block. I put on shoes and grabbed my keys from the hook by the door. It was June, the North Carolina humidity made the air soupy, brought with it an odd feeling of being alone inside your body, bounded by sweat, an astronaut in suburbia. I could feel sweat forming at the small of my back and above my lip before I was even to the intersection. I lived in a new neighborhood, which was a long oval loop with side streets running it like rib bones on a spine. The trees were still growing in from the clear-cut job the construction company had perpetrated, so there wasn't any escaping the sun. A lot of me hated this neighborhood, but I could afford it and then some, and I'd grown tired of renting in downtown Raleigh, and the house was cozy and well-built, and I was just getting to be this age of person.

The walk wasn't helping anything. I didn't want to not be myself, but also: I wanted to not be myself. It was more than a dead bird. It was everything. The back of my neck was damp. I pulled my hair up, looped it into the hair tie I kept around my wrist. A car went by, and the driver raised three fingers with his driving hand as a halfhearted wave. I nodded.

I could just bury the bird. It would be easy, and in some ways the right thing to do. Respectful at least. I thought of it. Even whole and alive, it wouldn't have been a pretty bird. It was all gray and white, with expressionless yellow eyes. Maybe it had a personality. Maybe it was loving, but how could something with a hooked beak and talons be loving? And what kind of a man loves a bird? What kind of man even takes it to heart when one dies? A bird dying is sad only in the immediate. It is not a tragedy with history or a future. Wherever Jeremy was, he'd be fine. And it was his fault his bird was loose in the neighborhood to boot. And where was Jeremy, anyway? I was starting to think he might be an asshole.

When I got around the block and back inside, the first thing I saw was the shoebox toppled to the floor. Baker was making happy growling noises from the office. I ran in there, leaving the front door open behind me. He didn't have the bird, though. He was lying in the middle of the room, gnawing on what was left of my shirt. I thought maybe he'd eaten the carcass, until I saw that he kept glancing up to the ceiling expectantly. I followed his gaze. The parrot was clinging to the lights of the ceiling fan, one wing hanging red and limp at its side. It watched me and Baker in turn, making little clicking noises to itself and bobbing its head along to nothing. Then it grabbed one of the tendons that hung limp from its body with its beak and pulled on it, ripping it free.

I backed up into the door frame. "Baker, come," I said, and he stood up immediately and left the room, dragging the bloodied shirt alongside. I shut the door.

I was no expert on birds, but it had died. It had entirely died. It had gone limp in my own hands. Plus the amount of blood I'd cleaned up was significant. Plus the way its body felt like it had no weight at all as I'd wrapped it in the shirt and placed it in the shoebox. How had it even made the flight into another room?

Where was fucking Jeremy?

I collected the shoebox. I picked up my bloodied shirt. Baker was sniffing around in the front yard, and I called him back in. I shut the door. These were things I knew to do, so I did them. When they were done, I sat on my couch and wept for the realization that I was entirely unprepared for most of the things that might happen in life. Baker licked the sweat from my calves.

There wasn't anything in the office that I needed. It was basically unused space in my home, full of boxes still packed after a year of living here and bins of crafting supplies for hobbies I'd had in college. I had no reason to go in there. I could let the bird have it as long as necessary.

From the office came a fluttering, a clatter of something smacking into the blinds, and then, loudly, *Where's Jeremy?*

"I don't fucking know!" Baker startled and went on a barking tear up and down the hallway. I let him. Everything was a little unglued with me. I thought about myself at a bar, later, telling this to my colleagues over drinks. What did I do next? What happened with the bird? And where was Jeremy?

In one version Jeremy was a good-looking guy about my age, and the bird had been something he'd got as a kid, and birds live a long time, and though he liked the bird he was a little bit over it, and when he came over and saw what was happening, he took it home and buried it properly in his yard and after a respectful amount of time I saw him mowing his yard and stopped to say hello, and it either ends there or else we get coffee and it either ends there or we go back to my place and it either ends there or we explore each other and find things we like and it either ends there or the bird becomes the kind of *how did you two meet* story that *oh, you won't believe, but it's true, I swear.*

In another version, Jeremy was a child still, and my action or my inaction on what would become of the bird didn't matter, because the bird left his life and entered mine and when it all was over the bird was either a broken monster or just a twice-dead bird.

In still another version, I nursed the bird back to health, feeding it from a dropper, stitching up its wing, and he and Baker became best friends and a viral sensation. Millions of likes on Facebook for their unlikely friendship. The bird would sit on Baker's paw, or nuzzle into his earflap while Baker slept. There'd be a little segment on morning television. And the bird's name was Jeremy, actually, not the owner's, who never appeared, anyway.

In another version, I got in trouble, real trouble, with the ASPCA and the city for not reporting the bird, as this kind of parrot was known to carry a rare disease, and Baker was quarantined for a month and then finally put down, and they sliced his brain into investigative chunks, and though they found nothing, they were just doing their due diligence, they're very sorry ma'am.

Or I did nothing, and the bird occupied my office, and I left it in there until the room was silent for some time, and I waited longer, weeks, months, through the buzzing of flies and the smell coming on and then fading, and after I would never get the carpet clean where the bird had last landed and gone to rot.

More clattering. Something hit the ground in the office. The story was not going to unfold in any of those nice or awful ways. Stories rarely do—they're there, then they're gone again before they have time to make sense.

Baker skidded into the shut door and jammed his muzzle under it as best he could. I loved that dog. He was my good boy. He backed off and scratched at the door, imploring. He looked back at me and whined, licked his lips.

I stood up and walked over to let nature run its course.

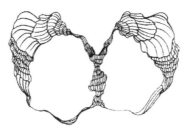

Everywhere in the house, little wind-up animals puttered and buzzed along wobbling arcs. They were made of plastic, filled with tin gears. Some of them breathed sparks from their jaggletooth mouths, or went on wheels, or stole coins when no one was looking, depositing them behind a houseplant for later. This is the way of small things.

The owner of the house presided over them from his place on the floor, youngish, handsomish, and alone. He imagined himself this way. Sometimes he would go online and buy a bulk box of the toys or bid on an older one he had an eye on. Mostly, though, he'd sit there or lie there, and when one of them came back to him he would pick it up, feel its movement in his palm, wind it to bursting, and send it off again. He did not believe any object that could move on its own had the capacity to be junk.

Once the owner of the house had wanted to kill himself, and then later he didn't want that. When he opened up to people about that time, he wished he had an answer as to why. Why, both feelings, wanting/not wanting. If he did, he might not be so afraid of feeling either of them again, of that slow, halting descent down or that effortful and possibly meaningless ascent up the ladder from the contentment he'd settled into, a contentment found easily, a contentment that comes when you twist a grooved plastic knob between thumb and forefinger, feel it click through as the spring tightens, store up a little bit of yourself in something very small and let it go.

175

CONCATENATION

A bunch of things are happening at once.

An infant that does not understand how differences of light and shadow affect the world believes his mother's face is constantly shifting in hue and shape. Still, he knows her as mother—in darkness, in light, in the echo-sprawl of the kitchen, in her worry of his too-dead sleep, in the garden they walk where she stoops with him to read the names of the different orchids, when she puts him down as he screams and it is just to have a brief moment of her own, when all else is confusion—mother.

A girl at a bus stop looks very tired, and a man walks up to her and apologizes to her for a thing he did to someone who was not her. This past week she dyed her hair a noticeable color, realizing too late that she does not like to be noticed after all. The man is adamant. She says *Okay, okay.* Neither feels absolved of anything real.

A man sits in a chair outside, his legs drawn up into the chair because of a nearby ant bed. He thinks about chocolate covered ants, how somewhere not in his backyard there is a factory that dips ants into a deep shining vat of chocolate, as if making them into a novelty could somehow counteract their base reality, could keep them from building their mounds on our lawns, over our graves. And then he thinks of how this practice is also tied to the cleaning up and sanitizing of tribal necessity—that is, the eating of ants is a thing that indigenous cultures somewhere probably still do for sustenance—and he thinks about how typical and sad that is of a Western society, to sweeten the things that are not our own, and he gets a little tired of thinking, so he puts his feet down again in the grass, let the ants do what they may.

And in a bathroom a mirror grows tired, too. Everything it shows is a little late, a little out of focus. The man who owns it brings people over to brush their teeth in front of it. They describe the experience as upsetting to anyone who will listen.

And somewhere else a woman comes across the word *wunderkammern* three times in one day and is struck a little dumb by the coincidence. She thinks it must be a sign of either something she's been left out of or of the world making something new and fully formed that day. And of course, the curious word means "cabinet of wonder" and refers to an old practice of having a designated place to store random and wonderful things, which seems a rather cruel idea for the world to have kept from her, or an even crueler thing for the world to have only just this day figured out should exist.

And a fish disappears with no explanation. One moment it is darting around a piece of coral, and the next moment it was never there at all. As though the world were just too tired to keep track of its existence on top of everything else.

And the palm of my own hand grows tired. I put a quarter on it and it falls through to the floor, heads up. Every time it is heads up, as the quarter has grown tired of having two faces.

Everyone wondered: "If the world has seams, what meaning can be found in one? To pluck those stitches free?" And then everyone replied: "If I was not so tired, I would pull with you."

By everyone, I mean me. Also you, if you like.

And in an office building the employees are asked to sit in cubicles and wear different masks carved from delicate porcelain. The Stoic Professional. The Happy Lunchtime. Gabbing With Jill Down The Hall. The schedule of masks is strictly regimented by people in floors high above them, in their own cubicles, wearing their own masks. It is the obvious thing to do, and also, for most, a relief. It is so difficult to wear your own face all the time, they think.

My friend writes a beautiful sentence, which I am reading at the same time as it is being written. We are both so tired.

A small dog falls into a drainage ditch. The walls of the ditch are concrete and about as high as a young child. If we are not out looking, if we are not lucky, the dog will starve long before we find it. So we are out there, looking, lucky. Can you believe it? Is belief enough?

By a bunch of things I mean everything. By at once I mean as one. I mean read this out of order, and scrawl your own stuff into the margins, mail me your own pages, think about the ways that what I am telling you is happening and is real is inherently different from the things you know are happening and real. Decide if that matters or doesn't.

ACKNOWLEDGEMENTS

The stories in this manuscript first appeared in the following publications, sometimes in slightly altered form: "Ali/Wendy" in *Georgia Review*, "The Father Makes a Mistake" in *Paper Darts*, "Guardianship" in *Smokelong Quarterly*, "Housewarm" in *Gold Wake Live*, "Interrogation" in *Yemassee*, "Liminal Domestic" in *Sundog Literature*, "The New Old West" in *cream city review*, "Nighthawk" in *XRAY Literary Magazine,* "Primogenitive" in *Atlas Review*, "Remainders" in *Beloit Fiction Journal,* "Scab" in *Split Lip Magazine,* "Who We Used to Be" in *Booth*, and untitled pieces in *Wigleaf, DIAGRAM, Menacing Hedge, Monkeybicycle,* and *The Forge.* Thanks to those journals and their editors for the trust, the home, and the good feedback (particularly that of Laura Citino, whose thoughtful reading helped break this book open).

Thanks to Régine, Jeremy, Courtney, April, Andy, Markie, Elise, Melanie, Josh, Erin, Justin, James, Colin, and many others for the friendship and support. Thanks to the friends in Ellensburg who kept me feeling normal when I needed it. Thanks to my people in DC for making me feel at home. Thanks to Bummer Club for teaching me that who I am is okay too (have fun crying!). Thanks to Courtney and Conor and everyone else at Spiderweb Salon for giving me space, for sharing your art, and for making life a little more worth the while. Thanks to Lemon for being a good dog. Thanks to Jaclyn for every single other good thing. And thanks, finally, to you. Yes, I mean you. I hope you found something you needed in here.

ABOUT GOLD WAKE PRESS

Gold Wake Press, an independent publisher, is curated by Nick Courtright and Kyle McCord. All Gold Wake titles are available at amazon.com, barnesandnoble.com, and via order from your local bookstore. Learn more at goldwake.com. Here are some of our recent titles:

Kyle Flak's *Sweatpants Paradise*
Melissa Barrett's *Moon on Roam*
Brandon Amico's *Disappearing, Inc.*
Dana Diehl and Melissa Goodrich's *The Classroom*
Sarah Strickley's *Fall Together*
Andy Briseño's *Down and Out*
Talia Bloch's *Inheritance*
Eileen G'Sell's *Life After Rugby*
Erin Stalcup's *Every Living Species*
Glenn Shaheen's *Carnivalia*
Frances Cannon's *The High and Lows of Shapeshift Ma and Big-Little Frank*
Justin Bigos' *Mad River*
Kelly Magee's *The Neighborhood*
Kyle Flak's *I Am Sorry for Everything in the Whole Entire Universe*
David Wojciechowski's *Dreams I Never Told You & Letters I Never Sent*
Keith Montesano's *Housefire Elegies*
Mary Quade's *Local Extinctions*
Adam Crittenden's *Blood Eagle*
Nick Courtright's *Let There Be Light*
Kyle McCord's *You Are Indeed an Elk, but This Is Not the Forest You Were Born to Graze*

ABOUT THE AUTHOR

Zach VandeZande is an author and professor. He lives in Ellensburg, Washington (sometimes) and Washington, DC (sometimes). He is the author of a novel, *Apathy and Paying Rent* (Loose Teeth Press, 2008), and of this book. His work has appeared in *Ninth Letter, Gettysburg Review, Yemassee, Georgia Review, Cutbank, DIAGRAM, Sundog Literature, The Adroit Journal*, and elsewhere. He knows all the dogs in his neighborhood. Find more of his work at zachvz.com

CPSIA information can be obtained
at www.ICGtesting.com
Printed in the USA
JSHW021509010819
1017JS00003B/14